blues
in paradise

a weekend of stories

by lou zitnik

Hilo, Hawai'i

Lou Zitnik Books and Movies
www.louzitnik.com

Publisher's Note: This is a work of fiction. Names, characters, places, and incidents are a product of the author's
imagination. Locales and public names are sometimes used
for atmospheric purposes. Any resemblance to actual people, living or dead, or to businesses, companies, events,
institutions, or locales is completely coincidental.

ISBN 978-0-9985504-1-1

Blues in Paradise/ Lou Zitnik – people's edition 2, 2017

Aloha

These are not Hawaiian stories. Not local or regional stories. They are a traveller's stories, written for restless people who long for a place to call home.

The stories and the characters are fictional, but even so, I stood with them in the shadow of volcanoes, searching the horizon for a paradise we could not reach.

I was born in Panama, the son of two Army veterans of WWII. We moved often, from army base to army base, and I continued that tradition of movement when I left home. North to college in San Francisco, then east to teach English in Kabul, Afghanistan, then west via Rome to coach swimming in the Dominican Republic, then to Pacifica, California. Every year or so, I went looking for a new place. Then I landed in Hawai'i.

Acknowledgements

The stories in this collection grew from more than twenty-five years of my experience living in Hawai'i, first on Maui, then Oahu, and finally the Big Island. They could not have been written without the help of my dearest friend and wife, Amy Self, and without the deeply moving experience of living in this place, these islands called Hawai'i.

Many of the stories were published in local literary magazines or in Hawaii's most widely read magazine, Honolulu Magazine. The list below identifies their first appearance, starting with the most recent of the.

"magic words in the palace of desire" runner-up in Honolulu Magazine Fiction Contest, 2006, published on Honolulu Magazine website.

"golden madonna" published as "Duct-Taped in Hilo," winner of 2005 Honolulu Magazine Fiction Contest.

"the language of nicotine," runner-up in 2004 Honolulu Magazine Fiction Contest.

"news crawling in hilo" published in part as "Postmodern Aloha Blues" in TinFish, 2001.

"fingertip chat" honorable mention in 2001 Honolulu Magazine Fiction Contest.

"working for jesus" published as "Poi Dogma" in Kanelehua, 2001.

"why i live in a tsunami zone" in Honolulu Magazine, winner of 1999 Fiction Contest.

"no outward signs" published in Makalii, 1998.

"a man has a right" in Chaminade Literary Review, 1997.

"high test blues" runner-up in 1996 Honolulu Magazine Fiction Contest.

"journal entries" in Bamboo Ridge, 1995, in Makalii. 1994.

"a case of mistaken identity" in Pleiades, 1993.

"haole boy" in Hawaii Review, Fall 1992.

"the price of real estate" runner-up in Honolulu Magazine Fiction Contest, 1992.

"remembering black granite" published as "Black Granite" in Hawaii Review, 1990.

"Cockfight Serenade" in Chaminade Literary Review, winner of John Unterecker Prize, 1990.

"falling for eddie" as "Crazy Eddie" runner-up in Honolulu Magazine Fiction Contest, 1988.

"home run" in premier issue of Chaminade Review, 1987.

Not included in this collection: "Outsiders" in Chaminade Literary Review 1991, honorable mention Honolulu Magazine Fiction Contest in 1991. "Concrete Heroes" in Makalii, 1995, honorable mention in Honolulu Magazine Fiction Contest, 1994. "John & Me" in Mauian, 1986.

About The Author

While writing to escape, Lou Zitnik has been paying his share of the bills by teaching at a small college, coaching a swim team, reporting on sports for a daily newspaper, leading Scuba tours, and marrying a pretty attorney. In between gigs, he attended the Writers Workshop at the University of Iowa (MFA) and the University of Hawaii (Ph.D). At the moment, which has lasted nearly forty years, he lives in Hawaii with his attorney and two cats.

Lou has published two other books: Most recently (2016) *My Daughter*, a novel of mystery and discovery, and *Magic Words in the Palace of Desire*, a novel about two cats and their search for the meaning of love and wasted food in movies

Contents

a weekend

1. golden madonna

friday night, the Golden Madonna appeared in Hilo.

Saturday morning, Papa Joe, backing out of his driveway, checking his cracked rearview mirror, saw golden arms outstretched. "Holy moley," he whispered. Felt a thud. And hit the brakes.

Tiny red birds fluttered from Papa Joe's avocado tree to his mountain apple tree and back again. What was he supposed to do? He reached for the glove compartment, shook his head, then squeezed out of the tiny pickup and limped to the tailgate. "Where the heck," he said, grabbing the Madonna under her arms and dragging her clear of the muffler, "did you come from?"

Golden eyes stared at the blue sky.

Gently, Papa Joe balanced the Madonna's golden feet on the asphalt. Who would do such a thing? Leave a statue in the middle of the street? Didn't people in this town ever forget? He touched the crack at the base of the Madonna's neck. Gently, he brushed bits of asphalt off her lips. His fingertips came away sticky golden.

***

Somewhere near the same moment, on a mist-slippery road between Volcano and Mountain View, Theresa Domingo pressed on the gas pedal of her 84 Stanza and yelled into her cell phone, "I love you!" She was headed down the mountain, after a 24-hour shift at the Aloha Aina Mana Bed and Breakfast, to work the breakfast rush at Blaine's. "I love you," she shouted. Then her Stanza flew into the air, hung there for a moment, crashed through a wall of bamboo, and slammed into a telephone pole.

"Holy mother of god," a tourist from Virginia said, crossing himself, running, wiping the morning rain from his face. The Stanza had landed on its back. "No one survived this one." Bracing his feet against the rusted metal, he peeled back what was left of the drivers-side window. A woman's hand drooped out, her bloody fingers still clutching a cell phone.

"Theresa? You there?" a man's voice asked. "Theresa?"

The tourist pried the phone out of her fingers and yelled into it, "Send an ambulance. Please. I'm..." He did not know where he was. "On the volcano road," he said. "The phone belongs to a woman. Send an ambulance." He felt Theresa's bloody wrist. Felt a faint pulse. "Hold on, dear," he managed to say. He did not know where to start. He wiped the blood from her arm, uncovering a homemade tattoo, the outline of a cross inked above Kona Girl.

Theresa's lips moved. The cell phone kept talking. "Kona double espresso," a man's voice said.

The tourist was crying, inhaling cold mountain air mixed with the smell of gasoline and ginger perfume. He did not know what to do. "Don't talk, dear. Save your strength," he said, touching Theresa's lips gently with his fingertips. "Be quiet now.

2

It'll be okay, honey." His fingertips came away covered with blood.

***

Papa Joe watched the woman's bright red fingernails pin his $5 bill to the counter. He didn't like to spend more than 50¢ on coffee, but today he needed Manny's help. "Double ex-large Kona," he said.

"Venti," the girl smiled.

"Howzit," Papa Joe answered. The woman laughed, and Papa Joe remembered a young woman like her, a wild haole girl with red hair and dangling earrings. This woman behind the counter could be her daughter. When she turned to get his coffee, her huge round pregnant stomach brushed against a tray of glasses. "Hard work being one mother," Papa Joe said.

The woman rubbed her belly and smiled, "Isn't he beautiful?" She pushed the $5 bill and a hefty mug of coffee across the counter. "Manny said he'd be out in a minute."

No ring on her finger. Women didn't need husbands these days, not even for having babies. Pretty soon they'd only need to take a pill. Papa Joe wondered why he could think of such crazy things, but when it came to a statue appearing in the middle of road, his mind refused to work. He left the money on the counter and sat next to the window, in a soft leather chair. When he lifted the mug to his lips, he smelled ginger perfume. The woman had left her scent on the cup handle. He sniffed it again, then set the cup down on the table. He was too old to be smelling yellow ginger. He had lived alone for twenty-five years, and smelling such things only made him feel more alone.

At the cash register, a fireman in a blue uniform shouted into his cell phone, "I love you. I really do."

Papa Joe closed his eyes and saw the young fireman balanced on a shaky ladder, escaping with a woman in his arms from a burning building. "But no can, no more, Theresa. I'm not the one."

Papa Joe opened his eyes and saw the fireman yelling into his cell phone as he grabbed a mug from the pregnant cashier. "I'm not the one!" The ladder collapsed, and for Papa Joe, suddenly, the world had become all too obvious.

***

The two police officers had to shout to he heard over the EMTs wheeling Theresa into the emergency room.

"Speeding," the tall cop yelled.

"Not according to the witness!"

Theresa felt a cool mist blowing her lover's words through the car window.

"Domingo," the EMT read from a driver's license spotted with bloody fingerprints. "Twenty-eight years old. Kiawe Street. No insurance card. No medical record."

Theresa wanted to tell them not to hurt her baby. She was late for the breakfast rush and her mouth wouldn't work. Where was he? He should be here. He's a good man, hard headed, like his father. Born again. Don't hurt my baby.

"Any drugs in the car?"

"Nothing."

"She busted up pretty good."

"A hundred, maybe two hundred stitches."

"At least," the tall cop said. "Who knows what else."

***

Papa Joe threw the blanket off the Madonna.

"Holy moley," Manny said, crossing himself. He had stopped going to church a year after he graduated St. Joe's Elementary, but he still knew the moves. Hadn't he crossed himself three times before winning the Revolving 7s Jackpot in Vegas?

Papa Joe stuffed his hands in his pockets.

4

"That's one weird statue," Manny said. "Like you get one body in your truck."

"Her neck's cracked," Papa Joe said, thinking of his first welding torch. He pressed his thick index finger against the crack. "If she were made of metal, I could fix her."

"Things aren't right," Manny said, "when people leave a statue in the middle of the road."

Both men nodded their heads, both thinking of Papa Joe's tiny cul-de-sac and the night twenty-five years ago when Papa Joe had run down the statue in front of Mother Mary Star of the Sea Church.

"Has to be outside agitators. Your neighbors too old to be leaving statues in the middle of the road, unless maybe old man Pacheco. He crazy religious kine."

"Why would a religious person leave a statue in the road?"

"Religious people do all kine crazy things. Me, I had one auntie, crying all the time for her avocado tree that nevah give fruit. Huge that tree but no fruit. Then she seen a statue like this one for $5 at the Buddhist temple rummage sale. Had black mold all over. She rubbed it clean with bleach and stuck it in her yard, facing that avocado tree. Then she prayed to that statue for grow avocados. Oh please, god, give me avocados."

Papa Joe saw a golden cross held in a young woman's shaking fingers.

"The next day, that tree get plenty big kine juicy fruit. Ono. Buttery. My auntie, she took the fruit round to her neighbors, bragging about how buttery and juicy they was and about her statue and her miracle."

"No such thing as miracles," Papa Joe said.

"Did I tell you this story before? Anyway, you right. The next day that statue disappears. I think maybe some kid stole it. And everything goes to do-do. The avocado tree stops giving fruit.

Then the leaves fall off, nothing left but a skeleton. Like thunder hit it. Completely dead." Manny crossed himself three times.

Papa Joe tossed the blanket over the Madonna. "Me, I'm taking it to the dump. Can't be fooling around with a statue when I'm supposed to work the late shift."

"You can't take a statue of the Madonna to the dump. You already get marks against you. Remember. This deja...you know."

"Last time I meant to hit the statue."

"Wait. I get one idea. I'll fix it, and after work you take it to the cemetery. Can always use another statue at the cemetery."

***

Through the window, Theresa saw mango trees circling, felt herself drifting, the earth moving on wheels, felt her baby's heart beating, tasted copper, smelled disinfectant, felt the light from the window turn dark, and heard the nurses pass, chatting about coffee and an old man who was an absolute saint of an angel.

She closed her eyes, wished deep inside for something good to happen, and when she opened them, saw the absolute saint of an angel standing in the doorway, a halo of golden light outlining his blazing head of glory. In his hand, he held a mighty spear. When he stepped forward, the light came with him, and he appeared wise and brave, and only slightly bald.

In respectful whispers, Theresa spoke her heart. "Why would god do this to me? You're one angel, you should know why god would hurt a woman and her baby. I'm one hard-working woman. Why put a woman on this earth, give her one man, let her feel him inside her, and then take the baby? You one saint. Tell god to take me, leave my baby."

Papa Joe moved closer to the bed. His job was to clean floors. Each night he mopped one mile of green tile. Sometimes, a patient would call to him and he would go in to talk or listen, to help take away the emptiness, but never in this room. He had

6

been in it only once, twenty-five years ago. Tonight, though, he had heard the woman crying.

"Give me one god who doesn't hurt people," Theresa whispered.

Papa Joe did not know what to say. In this room he had sat next to his wife, holding her hand, in this hospital, watching her die, taking their only child with her, still holding the gold cross in her hand.

"One gentle god, like Mother Mary," Theresa said.

Papa Joe watched the woman's lips move. He leaned his mop against the wall, and sat in the chair next to her bed. He saw the woman's hand, the tattoo on her arm.

"See," he said, rolling up his shirtsleeve, revealing his tattoo of a bulldog. "That's a devil dog, the Marine mascot."

The woman stared at the ceiling, whispering, "Mother of God, please help."

He wanted to say something, but he had fought in Vietnam and worked ten years in the shipyards in Oakland, and in all that time, he had never seen god help anybody. "I found one Madonna today. Found it under my truck. Manny, he knows how to fix things, and he told me statues like this one can do miracles. Me, I'm one welder, and I'm only good at welding metal, but Manny he tells me this Madonna can grow avocados."

"Mother of God, please help."

Papa Joe took her hand. It felt smooth and soft and warm like his wife's hands, the way they always felt in his dreams.

"People call me Papa Joe because I used to take care of the kids in the neighborhood. They're all grown up now. I live alone." He did not want to tell the woman the whole story because then he would have to tell her how his wife and baby had died in this room, and how he had gone crazy and run down the

Mother of Jesus in front of Mary Star of the Sea Church. "Me, I was one welder, if it was metal I could fix it."

They passed the night together like that, Papa Joe holding her hand and watching her lips for signs of life and telling her that Tungsten Inert Gas was a welding process that joined metals by heating them with a tungsten electrode that should not become part of the completed weld.

He told her about his lychee tree, the only one in Hilo that gave fruit, and the cactus plant in his driveway, the two cats who visited from next door, and how he kicked the crap out of Manny on New Years because Manny had used duct tape to fix his mailbox.

***

Sunday morning, the two nurses found Theresa breathing comfortably.

Like one miracle.

The spray-painted Madonna was standing in the corner. When one of the nurses tried to move her, the statue's head wobbled, and the nurses noticed the duct tape around her neck.

"A golden Madonna," said the nurse from New York, who up to that moment thought she had seen everything.

"Bandaged with duct tape," said the nurse from Hilo.

They both laughed.

"Has to be Manny Matos done this. Went to elementary with him, and he always stay fixing everything with duct tape."

As Papa Joe backed his tired, old truck out of the hospital driveway, the nurse from New York laughed so hard she thought she was going to pee her pants. And Theresa felt her baby move, heard her heart beating, and knew life was coming, soon.

friday

2. falling for eddie

---

eddie liked to talk.

That was his problem, that and a couple other things, but the big problem was his mouth. He couldn't keep it shut. I warned Eddie, told him to be careful, but he didn't listen. He wasn't good at listening.

The first time I saw Eddie, I was working the graveyard shift and he showed up all young and smiley in his new aloha shirt, blue slacks, and rubber slippers and told me that he's from back east, he's been working the day shift for about six months, and now they want him to try the night shift. Oh, yeah, and his family knew Old Lady Pline. That's why he got the job, but I shouldn't hold that against him because he went to Yale and he's willing to work 24 hours a day, 7 days a week, 388 days a year, to get the job done.

Me, I had gone to community college for three years, and my family didn't know anybody, not even me. We were separated. As for working 24 hours a day to get the job done, I like getting

---

the job done but a lot faster than 24 hours. I guess you could call me a union man.

Eddie whipped a cigarette from his pocket and pointed it at the coffee machine. "Mind? I live on coffee and cigarettes." He stopped talking long enough to show me his tobacco-stained fingers. "You have to pay for your pleasures. Sometimes, if I'm really hungry, I'll eat a Milky Way for the vitamins." His head rolled back, his nicotine-stained teeth flashed, and he laughed himself into a coughing fit. Not a pretty sight.

"Don't worry about me," he said, finally calming down. "Me, I've been checking the place out. Working courts and government." He sucked on the cigarette. "I got a line on things. He took a second to exhale. "Can I ask you a question?"

I was about to say no, but he kept right on rolling.

"Do you gamble?" he asked. "Pline wants me to write about gambling. Hey, if that's what she wants. She's the boss."

The publisher in those days was Nora Pine, a half-senile old ghost who drank diet soda by the case and stopped by once a week to pretend she was in charge. Her money came from way back, from land her family had weaseled out of the Hawaiians. Now they had it in pineapples and sugar cane and hotels, or were selling it off inch by inch at a million dollars a pop. No gambling there.

Eddie sucked on his cigarette. He was 25, maybe, but he sounded older. "Hell, gambling," he said, "everyone gambles. Not Pline, though. She's a missionary. No fun allowed. But if she wants me to cover gambling, I'll cover gambling."

The phone rang, and Eddie picked it up. He was that quick.

"Yeah, city desks, Maui Tribune, this is Eddie. No, tell me." He dragged on his cigarette, sipped at his coffee, looked at me. "I can talk. Yeah. Sure." He pointed his cigarette at me. "I can trust you, right?"

To him, it was a joke. Ha, ha.

"Yes, okay," he said. "I'll be there in twenty minutes." He smiled at me with his stained teeth. "See, put me on nights and look what I get. See."

I didn't see anything.

"My people know where to find me. That was my guy in planning department. He wants to talk. He knows something about the Makena condo deal."

Back then everyone knew something about the Makena deal but no knew anything. It was a same-old story. A resort project had been proposed for one of the last undeveloped beaches in Kihei. Permits had been requested and greased, pissed-off letters to the editor written, lawsuits filed, and testimony at public hearings ignored. The deal kept rolling. Now, no matter what, a few people were going to make a lot of money. There'd be more jobs, more small business, and only one less beach for fishermen and nude sunbathers, neither one of whom had much of a lobby.

Eddie started up his coughing, and I thought maybe he was going to cough up his insides, but he took another hit off his cigarette and recovered enough to say, "This is big."

"Sure."

"This guy says he has a list of all the hui's that are holding land along the road leading to the hotel. He claims the godfather of the syndicate is involved, owns a piece in his wife's name."

For a smart fast-talker, Eddie didn't know much. "One of those calls comes in every night," I said. "Everyone on Maui thinks they know the godfather of something."

Eddie hacked away with his cough. The only thing strong enough to stop him was a big gulp of coffee. "And what do you do?"

"Ignore them."

"You're sick."

"Even if there was a godfather, what are you going to do? Beat him over the head with a typewriter?"

"Say, how long have you been a journalist?"

He tossed the cigarette in the trash, lit another one. Standing next to him was like standing next to a jittery nuclear reactor. I was waiting for the explosion that would leave what was left of me glowing for twenty thousand years. For a second, he stood there waiting for answer, his cigarette in his mouth, letting the ashes drip down his shirt. Apparently, he wasn't one for neatness. It was past midnight, and I heard a siren tearing down Kaahumanu Avenue.

"Me, I'm going to follow this lead." He pointed the cigarette at me. His brown fingertips handled the job like seasoned professionals. "I'm driving out to Haiku and meet this guy."

"He wants to meet you in the country? At night?"

"So what?"

If, like some people told me later, Eddie was so smart, why did he ask stupid questions? "Leave it alone," I said. "Don't go looking for something you don't want to find."

That was my try at advice, but, like I said, Eddie wasn't any good at listening. He was already headed for the door, taking his camera and notepad with him. "You're wrong," he shouted at me. "It's the only thing that can save me."

What the hell that meant, I don't know. As it turned out, he couldn't have been more wrong, because Monday morning he turns up at the bottom of a cliff out Nahiku way. The police called it an accident because there's alcohol in his blood, what was left of it, and the ground was wet, so they figured he slipped, accidentally, right down a fifty-foot drop to the rocks below. No sign of struggle, no nothing, just a body by the ocean. A tough way to die, but what way isn't?

My luck, I was the last one to see him alive, or so the cops thought, so I had to spend a couple of hours telling them what I knew, which was nothing. Then the city editor, Noah Smith, called me in and said I knew Eddie pretty good. Which wasn't true, but why argue? Smith didn't like arguments. Physically, he wasn't imposing, unless maybe big and sloppy is imposing, but he had a nasty coke habit and a bad temper, and he had stabbed a couple of reporters in the back. Not that they didn't deserve it. Up to then I had stayed out of his way by working the graveyard, for three years.

Anyway, he was sitting behind his desk in his under-sized aloha shirt and looking at me like he was wondering who the hell I was and how much could he trust me. After getting me straight, he said that as far as he was concerned Eddie was a dead story, which in my opinion was a poor choice of words. He said that Pline had a hair up her nose about this guy, Eddie. She wanted something, something that would make him and the paper look good.

"How can a drunk slipping down a cliff make the paper look good?" I asked.

Smith shrugged his shoulders. "That's your problem. Pline knew his father, so say something nice. Make it up if you have to. You worked with him."

"One night."

"That's plenty. Anything special happen that night?" He was checking the notes on his desk. "He say anything to you?"

"Nothing."

"No calls?"

"Nothing."

"He just walks off at the end of his shift, goes for a midnight walk out in the boonies, and slips?"

"Sounds like the story."

"Write it," he said. "I'll put it on a back page. You know, for Pline. Focus on his college stuff, his family, and potential, a tragic accident. Understand? Do a good job and I'll take you off graveyard."

"Sure," I understood. I walked out of his office and bumped into Roy Matsui, a college intern running copy to composing for the 10:30 deadline. He looked bright and cheery, like a kid carrying roses to his prom date.

"You writing about Eddie?" he asked.

"Word gets around."

"This is his file."

"He had a file?"

"Employment file." He slapped a manila folder into my hand. "That's his girl. There, on the third line."

There were no relatives listed, only a woman's name in the space for person to notify in case of an emergency. This was the emergency.

"She's an artist," Roy said.

"How do you know?"

"I met her at a party."

"What party?"

"Eddie's birthday party."

"No one told me about a party."

"You work graveyard."

Hell, they could've asked. "Local girl?"

"No, but she looks local. She's got a place out past Haiku, a studio, Eddie slept there sometimes."

"He told you that?"

"Sure. Eddie told me lots of stuff. That guy could talk. See the address." He tapped a perfectly clean finger on the file.

"Yeah."

"Notice anything?"

"It's in the boonies."

16

"It looks pretty darn close to where Eddie slipped."

"Smith know that?"

"Who knows? He just told me to get the file and pass it to you."

"Eddie say anything else about the girl?"

"She had killah eyes."

If Roy was smart, he'd learn from Eddie's mistakes. Me, I could've written the story by phone, but I needed a drink, so I nursed my Tercel past the airport, picked up two 16-ounce Buds at the 7-11 in Paia, and followed the twisting road to Haiku.

Five miles out of Paia, I found her mailbox on the ocean side of the highway, next to a dirt road that disappeared into a think bank of eucalyptus trees. The road was wide enough for a motorcycle. I spent ten minutes sliding through curves and dodging tree limbs. A cop car coming up from the ocean nearly knocked me into a ditch, but I managed to find her house, a redwood A-frame, at the end of a muddy driveway. The house looked like it belonged in the mountains in California, where the roof would keep the snow off. It faced the ocean, and had a screened in porch and a shed for a generator, which was upscale for Haiku. In those days, a lot of people in Haiku just parked their cars under a tree and set up camp, if they had a car.

Somehow I managed to get to the door without sinking into the mud. Music, classical stuff, was playing in the background. I knocked. Knocked again. The violins stopped and I heard her feet coming at me. When the door opened I didn't say anything.

"Yes?" she said.

Roy was right. She had killah eyes, even if they were a little watery, like she had been crying. But she wasn't crying now and she wasn't going to cry. There was almost six feet of her, wearing a red silk shirt and tight jeans. The shirt was see-through, and I wanted to see through the jeans, except looking at her like that made me feel kind of funny, because of Eddie.

"You lost?" she asked. She stood there with one hand in her pocket and one arm blocking the door, relaxed looking, waiting. I told her my name and where I worked and how I had come to write something about Eddie.

"Eddie," she said.

Her face didn't move much. I felt like I was standing at the edge of a cliff waiting for her to push me. "People down at the paper are pretty broken up about him being lost." In those days I was good at lying.

"He isn't lost."

"Sure."

She stood back and let me in. As I walked by her, I smelled ginger perfume, just a little, and it didn't seem right to me, her wearing perfume so soon after Eddie had taken a dive off a steep cliff. But who am I to complain?

The living room was big and airy, all cedar and picture window and fireplace. I sank into a leather couch that stretched across middle of the room. She sat on a stool behind an easel "It's a beautiful day," she said, as if she really meant it. It seemed a strange thing to say. When your boyfriend dies, you don't go around talking about beautiful days or wearing see-through silk shirts.

"Sure," I said, still fumbling. I pointed at the painting on the wall. "I like the sunflowers."

"That's Eddie's" She picked a piece of charcoal from a small wooden box. "I did it for him because he liked van Gogh. Do you like van Gogh?"

"I know the name."

"He was passionate and self-destructive, a dangerous combination."

The self-destructive part fit Eddie. "It's funny, but I never thought of Eddie as a guy who liked art. He never talked about art."

She didn't bite; instead, she asked me if I wanted something to drink. I said yes, if she had a beer, but she didn't. No surprise. "Water?" she asked. "Wine?"

I shook my head. Damn, she looked good brushing her hair back and looking out the picture window. Off in the distance, the ocean was a blue strip fading into the sky

"The police haven't come by yet," she said.

"Why would they?"

"I was the last one to see him alive. He was here that night."

She looked maybe thirty, or thirty-five, or twenty-five. It was impossible to tell, she was that kind of babe. What the hell had she seen in Eddie?

"Eddie believed in being a reporter," she said. "It meant everything to him." She went back to work on her canvas, and I went back to work on her. "That's okay if you get good stories. Trouble is, most of the stories I get aren't interesting. Eddie, he got some interesting stories."

"Did Eddie ever tell you why he came to Hawaii?"

"Not really."

"It's funny," she said. "He was like a lot of other people. He was looking for paradise. That was the wonderful thing about him. He believed in paradise. He drank too much and smoked too much, but he believed that if he worked hard enough, he could help create paradise. Do you believe in paradise?"

I was good at lying but not that good. "No, not really."

"Neither do I.," She worked the charcoal into the canvas, her hand moving up and down in quick little sweeps as the sunlight shifted back to shadows.

"Did he say anything that made you think he was depressed?"

She worked that charcoal like she had a deadline to meet, keeping her eyes on the canvas and her hand moving. "When he was tired, he let the world get inside him, but he wasn't suicidal if that's what you mean."

"An accident, well, it's tough way to go."

"You believe that?"

"What?"

"That it was an accident?"

"Why not?"

"Are you really from the newspaper?"

"Sure. I worked with Eddie. I work the desk mostly, but I'm a reporter"

"Then you must know."

"Know what?" The conversation was making seasick.

"The night he died, he was going to see a man who worked for the county about a story. It had something to do with one of the people at the newspaper."

Jeez, she was way out of my league.

"Would you like to see what I'm working on?"

I really didn't care one way or the other, but I took a look, just to keep her happy. She had charcoaled Old Lady Pine and a Japanese guy, one of the money guys, with Makena Beach in the background.

"Eddie wanted me to do it. He said it was for the story, the one he was working on. Would you like it?"

Like I said, she was way out of my league. She handed me the drawing, and I rolled it up, and said something about going back to the office. I didn't want her to show me to the door, nothing. I just wanted to get out. Funny how someone as beautiful as her can make a guy feel scared.

Back at the office, I sat in front of my terminal, staring at the rolled up drawing, thinking that if anybody saw it, Eddie's girl would meeting him for pau hana drinks. I was typing in a paragraph about Eddie coming from Yale and being a hard worker and being too young to die at twenty-five when Smith appeared. Leaning over my shoulder, checking out the orange letters on the word processor.

"That's it?" he said.

"That's it."

"Roy said there was a girl."

I figured Roy wasn't learning anything in college, so I said, "She broke up with Eddie three weeks ago. No one has seen her since. You know how it is. People get lost."

"What's that?" he asked, pointing at the rolled up drawing.

"A van Gogh."

He smiled. At least, I figured it was a smile because his teeth were showing. "Where'd you get it?"

"At a flea market in Paia. The guy said it was an original."

That made him laugh. Why, I don't know. But he didn't look at the charcoal drawing and he didn't ask any more questions. "Print what you got," he said, walking away. "It's more than he deserves."

Anyway, that's how I got off the graveyard shift...the first time.

3. a man has a right

the day after Shinamura disappeared, the detective from Tokyo arrived. At least, he said he was from Tokyo, but he wasn't like any Japanese from Tokyo I had ever seen. And believe me, I've seen plenty. Working on Maui, I couldn't help but see plenty. Japanese money was everywhere.

Back in those days, the newspaper had its offices in an old Quonset hut left over from WWII. When Shebai found my office in the back, where they stored the asbestos, he had to bend over to keep from scraping his head on the doorway. I had seen plenty of big Japanese guys. Being six-two wasn't what made him not fit.

He nodded, like most of them do, not quite a bow, and offered me his hand. For a big man, he had soft skin and a comfortable handshake. Underneath though I felt tough muscles. Strictly class. When he told me the name of the company he worked for, I was impressed. As far as I was concerned, a Tokyo investigator riding high on big corporation yen had just as much right as me to make a living. Just don't lie to me in the process.

"You're wasting your time," I said. "The police are doing everything they can to find Shinamura."

"No doubt," he said, and without asking parked his linen shirt and faded blue jeans and $2,500 Swiss watch in my war surplus chair. The local cops had been through a hundred times looking for Shinamura and his rented Corvette. Even the Japanese Embassy had sent over a guy in a linen suit to ask, "Where is Shinamura?" Like, me, a sports writer in a t-shirt and canvas shorts was supposed to know? Nobody could find him, no matter how hard they looked, not even after his family offered a $20,000 reward.

"I'll tell you what I told the cops. I saw him once, at the windsurf contest his company sponsored, then he disappeared. People do that on Maui, come and go. You know, here today, gone to Maui."

"No doubt."

"What the hell's the big fuss? Shinamura is over twenty-one. Heck, he's over fifty-one. If he doesn't want to go home, he's got a right. Give him a break. If he wants to fly off to Aruba with a windsurf babe, let him."

"In this matter," he said slowly, as if he had practiced the line a couple of hundred times, "my loyalties are not to Shinamura."

That sounded like a line from a movie, an old Samurai film.

"I am looking for a woman," he said.

"Aren't we all?"

Gently, he slid two 3x5 black-and-whites out of his leather briefcase and pushed them across the desk to me. From a background of sand and ocean, a babe squeezed into a pink one-piece smiled. In the next shot she was rigging a slalom board with Shinamura's help. She looked as happy as a deaf guy at a Karaoke bar.

"A friend of yours?"

"Do you recognize her?"

Hell, yes I knew her. It was Eddie's old girlfriend. It was easy to imagine her sailing nude over a glassy smooth ocean. It was easy to imagine lots of things. The air conditioner was broken, but Shabai wasn't sweating. "No," I said. "Never seen her. She one of yours?"

"It is plain that she is not a Japanese national."

That's what pisses me off about Japanese guys. They take one look, and they think they can tell real from local. My family was California, sure, but I'm still Japanese — on the outside. I look Japanese, right?

"My apologies if I have offended you, Mr. Kawabata."

"No sweat."

Gently, he placed an envelope on my desk. "Consider this an advance."

My, my, he understood Americans. The hundred dollar bills inside felt crisp and new. "And the reward? The ten grand?"

"That money is no concern of mine."

Fine, but he wasn't from Tokyo.

It took us thirty minutes to drive out past the airport to Paia, to Mama's Fish Joint. The little restaurant was packed with Japanese, Canadians, Frenchies, English, Tahitians, South Africans, even a couple of locals. Very cosmopolitan. Most of them were washing down the $3.99 Ono special with $6 German beer. The fish was dry. The beer killah. After two mugs, I felt as if I had know Shabai for a long time. He was a good drinker. Between gulps, he kept his back straight, eyes clear, checking and rechecking every face in the crowd. For $500 I figured he deserved a guided tour of the hot spots. Nothing more. "You drink a lot of beer in Japan?"

"I enjoy beer."

"This beer, it's strong, right?"

"No doubt. A good beer, Mr. Kawabata." He gulped down another beer. "We make a similar beer in Japan. Do you know the history of brewing in Japan?"

"Sure. I know everything about Japan." Hell, I hardly knew anything but I look Japanese, right, so I'm supposed to know.

The waitresses were all windsurfers, working nights so they could sail during the day. Most of them were babes with buff bodies, short hair, and clean smelling skin. One of them, Gina Sato, had escaped from a ballet company. Without asking, she left two giant mugs of German lager at our table. When she and her perfume faded into the cigarette smoke, I said, "You Japanese go crazy over her type, am I right?"

"What type is that, Mr. Kawabata?"

"Hapa. Part Japanese, part haole."

"What is a haole?"

"White. American or French or something."

"I see."

"You don't see."

I gulped down half my beer. "Lots of island girls like her end up working for modeling agencies, for you guys."

"I do not concern myself with modeling agencies."

"But you find her attractive?"

"Why is that important?"

"Because she knew Shinamura." Before he could squeeze out of the booth, I grabbed his arm. "Be careful. Gina's good people. Everyone needs a little extra money and Maui is a hard place to pay rent, so she escorted Shinamura for a few nights. That's all. The police questioned her and she didn't tell them anything. No rough stuff."

"You offend me, Mr. Kawabata."

"Maybe I've been watching too many movies."

"Hollywood movies."

"What other kind is there?" I figured that Gina was safe. She didn't know anything and she knew how to keep her mouth shut, so I checked out the two babes perched behind me. Both of them were moonlighting to make ends meet, a couple of mainland girls in their early thirties, draped in black silk, with their thick hair brushed back, expensive gold earrings highlighting the soft skin of their cheeks. They looked good, too good. The tall one was Yoko, the short one Machiko. Like I said, sooner or later I get to know most everybody. It's a small island.

"Is your friend a businessman?" the tall one said.

"Yakuza."

Both women shook their heads. "Impossible," they purred.

"Why?"

"Yakuza are horrible dressers."

"With tattoos,: the short one said. "He's too adorable."

"A sweetie."

"He says he's from Tokyo," I said.

They both laughed. "No," the tall said. "He's from Osaka."

"I've always wanted a man from Osaka."

"What's so special about Osaka?"

"Men from Osaka are very traditional, moody, intense."

"How would you know?"

They were giggling when Shabai came back, but as soon as he sat down, they toned it down to a whisper. "Those two behind us are looking for trouble," I said.

"I am not interested."

"Why not? Look at them. They're beautiful."

"No doubt." He was looking at one of those maps the rental car companies give to tourists to help them get lost.

"What, you don't like aggressive women?"

"A moment please, I am having difficulties."

26

"No matter what the difficulties, I'm sure these two will oblige."

"No doubt. But a moment..."

"You need more beer, right? That's the Japanese way. Get so drunk you can blame it on the beer. Talk about repression. Three or four more beers and you'll be talking about whips and chains. That's big in Tokyo, right?"

"You are a strange man, Mr. Kawabata."

"Don't be so harsh."

"My disinterest is of a practical nature." He slid a wrinkled napkin across the table. "The young woman gave me this address."

"She gave you this?" It was an address buried so deep in the rain forest out Haiku way there was no way he was going to find it on a map. I had been there once before, a couple of days after Eddie showed up dead, at the bottom of a nearby cliff. "How?"

"I simply told her that I was in love with the woman in the picture. We were supposed to be married, and the old man in the picture had bought her away from me. Now, I needed to see her, to beg for her hand."

"And she believed you?"

"Romantic love is a concept greatly appreciated in the west."

This guy really had been watching a lot of movies. "And the map?"

"That is where you come in, Mr. Kawabata."

It's funny what a guy will do for five hundred bucks and a chance at ten thousand more. I guess it's better than working the modeling agencies. I followed the Hana Road along the coast, slowly rising and falling. Then I turned left, into the rain forest country at the base of the volcano. After a hundred turns, I lost track of time and direction. The trees blotted out the stars. A cool wind blew in through the window. We were drowning in darkness. At the last second when I thought I was going to suffocate in black, I saw a light, a circle of yellow beneath the moon. Shabai turned off the headlights as we glided to a stop.

"We will wait here for a moment," he said. From his briefcase, he produced a silver flask, poured a shot in a silver cap. "Sake, Mr. Kawabata?"

"No doubt."

"You are playing with me. Drink the sake and forget the idiosyncrasies of my vocabulary."

"Idiosyncrasies? My what a big word." The sake went down smooth. "Osaka. You're from Osaka?"

"Have you been to Osaka?"

"Only in a book."

"Mr. Kawabata, you have lost touch with your culture."

"What's new."

"You will die lonely, Mr. Kawabata."

"It's better than nothing."

He poured me another shot while mosquitoes waited outside the windows. "You cannot find Japan in books, Mr. Kawabata."

"No kidding?" Gee, really, Mr. Wizard. My head was spinning. His sake made German beer taste like soda water. He poured me another shot. "What will happen to her?" I said.

"You are concerned?" He twisted the cap onto the flask. "I am surprised, Mr. Kawabata."

I couldn't move. He had slipped me a sleeper, something strong and quick, something new and Japanese, but I was awake enough to inside his briefcase, airline tickets to Brazil and a nickel-plated .38.

"No harm will come to her," he said. "Believe me."

What choice did I have? I heard the car door shut, saw him walk slowly through the darkness. He had taken the gun. He knocked once, and when the door opened, I saw her by firelight, in a white silk blouse that reached her knees. She stood in the doorway for a long moment, then leaned forward and threw her arms around his neck, kissed him so hard I could feel it. The next thing I knew, they had disappeared inside.

Somehow, I managed to crawl out of the car, and ricocheted from tree to tree, to the front porch, crawled along the wall to the light in the window. In the sake zone, I pressed my face against the glass. Inside, a ceiling fan weaved currents of thick night air over orchids, a vase, a circular rosewood table, a pile of books, and bamboo mats.

She was sitting with her back to me, the blouse pulled down, exposing her shoulder blades. Her hair looked like waves. The muscles in her back reminded me of cage birds trembling and tigers in city streets. He was leaning forward, closing the distance to her lips. It was an odd way to be searching for Shinamura.

The last thing I remember was tasting her lips. They tasted of golden light and white orchids, ocean sounds and currents of cool air. Then I slipped and fell onto a narrow path through a haunted valley, crashed through a bamboo forest covered with mist. My feet sank in wet mud that smelled of ginger plants and rotting ohia. I saw her beneath the waterfall, saw the soft swelling of her breasts as she inhaled. Drops of water clung to her creamy skin as I stepped to the edge of the cliff.

***

The next morning, I managed to dig my face out of the mud and crawl back to my Toyota, where I found Shinamura handcuffed to the back door. Two days later, the detective from Tokyo arrived with my check.

He was like all the rest, all business in a black suit, tie, and a platinum Seiko watch. To top off the cliché, he was in a hurry. Definitely from Tokyo. He nodded, almost a bow, like they all do, and offered me his manicured hand. "You have been of great assistance to the Shinamura family, Mr. Kawabata."

"No doubt."

"You will be happy to know that Mr. Shinamura has returned safely to Tokyo." He tossed a 3x5 black-and-white on my desk. Eddie's girlfriend looked even better in this one. It's funny how a smaller bathing suit will do that for a girl. The detective from Tokyo tapped her forehead. "We are most interested in finding her. Mr. Shinamura has offered a substantial reward. Twice the money you hold in your hand. This is a delicate matter, not one for the police."

"What's the story?"

"Simply that Mr. Shinamura would like very much to talk to her."

"And Shabai?"

"He is no concern of ours, Mr. Kawabata, as long as he does not interfere."

I had a feeling that interfere was Shabai's middle name. "What's his connection to the girl?"

"No concern of yours."

No doubt.

From the picture, the woman and Shabai smiled up at me. So that's how he looked smiling. I imagined them in Brazil, dropping their rigs in the water. They would step onto the fiberglass decks, the wind would catch their sails, and off they'd go, white water splashing as they cut through the chop. Straight up the face of a wave they'd fly, for a moment hanging in midair.

"Do you know where she is, Mr. Kawabata?"

Twenty thousand is a lot of money, but, hell, it isn't everyday I get drugged by a romantic from Osaka who runs off to Brazil with Eddie's girlfriend. "No," I said. "No idea."

"She is a dangerous woman, Mr. Kawabata."

"No doubt." But a man has a right to live dangerously.

4. haole boy

i haven't seen Ernesto in thirty-three days, not since he ran away with the fry cook, but Friday afternoon he calls and says, "Big Johnny, I'm in trouble. Can you meet me at Kahului Harbor? By four? It's important." So I drive slow, real slow, and stop for coffee before I find him on the beach next to the loading docks.

It's after four. The sky is black with rain clouds, and the wind is blowing cold. None of this bothers Ernesto. He's wearing swim trunks and lifting an ama onto his bare shoulder. When I yell "Hey, haole boy!" he whips around so fast, the ama catches me hard on the elbow.

That doesn't faze him. No sorry, no nothing, just "You never change, right, brah."

I've only been on Maui a year but I already know a few local words. Brah means dude, and haole means white; it's pronounced "how-lee" but to me it sounds like "nig-ger." Ama doesn't count. Ernesto and me learned that means outrigger float back when we paddled canoes in San Francisco Bay.

"Did you think I was one of your local friends?" I say, rubbing my elbow. "Someone looking for a fight?"

He pretends not to hear. He does that when he doesn't want to argue. We never argued before we cam to Maui; now that he's Mr. Local we argue all the time. "Welcome to paradise," he says. The sad thing is, he means it. To me, Kahului Harbor is no paradise. It's on the wrong side of the island, where the wind starts blowing at noon and doesn't stop until sunrise next morning. You'd think that with all that wind, the air would smell good. It doesn't. It stinks of sewage.

"You're late," Ernesto says.

Two container ships are unloading at the docks. Workers shout into the wind as a forklift backs away, warning bell clanging. Outside the harbor the ocean is brown and gray and green and ugly.

"I was afraid you'd leave me hanging," he says.

A wave hits the breakwater, explodes in a thousand pieces and the wind carries the spray over the flat oily water. The air smells of sewage, salt, rust and diesel fuel. I make Ernesto wait. "You know me," I say. "Anything for a friend."

He smiles that stupid smile of his, like I said something funny, then he balances the ama on his shoulder and marches across the dirty sand, toward an canoe under an ironwood tree. Ernesto has thick shoulders, and he's a strong buggah, but by the time he reaches the canoe, sweat is dripping down his back and he's breathing hard. Still, he treats the ama like it's made of glass. He slips it off his shoulder, sets it down on an old tire, and pushes the tire closer to the canoe.

The canoe isn't much to speak of. It's a weather-beaten koa, about forty feet long, a couple feet wide, dark brown. It looks even darker next to Ernesto's pale skin. "We call her Koa, after the wood," he says, rubbing his hand along the ama.

"How original."

"It means brave, fearless."

Like, I didn't know that. "You'd have to be brave to paddle in this old tub."

Ernesto stands up, pretending he didn't hear me, sweat dripping down his cheek. "A week ago Wailea Canoe Club challenged us to an iron-man race, to the navigation buoy and back. Seven miles, starting right after work. Willie turned up sick today. We called around and couldn't get anybody. You're our last hope, Johnny."

"Me?" I say, acting surprised. "You're depending on me?"

Ernesto bends over the canoe, like he's looking for something. "We need your help, Johnny," he says. "You could sit in seat five. No one says we got to win. We just got to compete."

"What's the point?"

Before he says anything, he grabs a plastic bucket and kneels down by the canoe, pulls a rubber strip out of the bucket and wraps it around the ama, and pulls it tight. "It's about being part of a family, about working together."

"Bullshit," I say. We've known each other for years. Hell, I know how much he loves winning. Besides, his family, what there is of it, is in San Francisco. He was supposed to fly back there two months ago, to finish college and get back to his girlfriend. I'm just about to remind him, when Poncho shows up.

He's wearing black swim trunks, a white T-shirt and tiny black sunglasses that make him look like a blind man. When he lifts his arm to wave, his stomach slips out from under his T-shirt. I've never known a fry cook who wasn't fighting the battle of the bulge.

"Howzit," he says, like it's the most natural thing in the world to see me on the beach in Kahului Harbor. He shakes my hand Mainland style, not like the locals do when they make a big deal out of nothing. "Glad to see you, Johnny," he says. Poncho is Filipino, a local guy, but he spent a year on the Mainland going to junior college so he knows how to talk to me without any of that pidgin stuff.

"Howdy," I say, making myself sound like a cowboy from Texas, squeezing his hand hard even though he's being gentle with mine. He's a big guy, two inches taller than me and outweighs me by seventy-five pounds but I'm not afraid of him. I could take him in a fair fight. I'd circle him and punch him in the gut until his heart gave out, if none of his local buddies gangee'd on me. Locals stick together when it comes to fighting guys from the mainland, and who knows what side Ernesto would take now that he has gone native.

Poncho and him shake hands and hug like locals do, like they haven't seen each other in years. Why make a big deal out of saying hello? Anyway, after they're through making love and Ernesto is back rigging the ama, Poncho pats me on the shoulder and says, "Good, you're going to help us."

I'm about to tell him what I think, when a rusty Toyota pickup pulls into the parking lost, and three local guys pile out. They walk across the beach knotted together, shoulder to shoulder, like a gang. Up close, I realize one of this girl, a skinny kind girl dressed like a guy, in a sweatshirt and trunks but a girl. Poncho tells me their names while each of them shakes my hand, mainland style. There's Kawika, Joey, and the girl, Malama. So what? I'm supposed to remember all that? What I remember is Kawika is a tough and wiry guy, with a flat stomach and wide shoulders. Him and Ernesto together look like a couple of spark plugs. There's a skinny guy, young, maybe seventeen, smoking a cigarette. Joey's a big guy, like Poncho, with

34

sleepy eyes, but when he shakes my hand, his fingers feel like nylon rope. Malama, I can remember. She's the girl with the boy's name, maybe nineteen or twenty, smoking a cigarette. When she shakes my hand, she tries to crush it. Her I understand.

The locals and Ernesto stand in a circle, talking about work, smiling, slapping each other on the back, hugging, while I stand there, trying to figure a way to tell Ernesto I'm not going to help his new friends. I don't like mob scenes, especially with guys who don't know how to be winners. When I can't take the buddy-buddy stuff any longer, I grab Ernesto's arm and pull him away from the group, but just then the friggin guys from Wailea show up. Instead of stopping in the parking lot, they drive their big Ford pickup, towing a bright yellow fiberglass canoe with two red stripes on its bow, right across the beach. Eight guys jump out and lift the canoe on their shoulders and carry it to the water's edge, and set it down gently on the sand.

No hello or nothing to us.

All of them are in pretty good shape, big haole guys, tall and wiry. No girls. I'm thinking that their canoe weighs around four hundred pounds, our Koa twice that. "Nice canoe," I say.

"Our canoe is forty years old," Ernesto says. "It's a traditional Hawaiian racing canoe."

I'm thinking about the night Ernesto asked me to sign a petition for a moratorium on hotel construction; he even asked the local guys behind the bar to sign it, which was kind of funny because the local guys got lots of friends working in construction. They know tourism pays the bills, and them signing Ernesto's petition would have been like bartenders joining AA. The local guys laughed and told Ernesto that he was trying to be more Hawaiian than the Hawaiians. That's Ernesto. Always getting carried away

"That canoe is ready to fall apart," I say, "And look at those guys. They're tough. In shape. No girls."

"That's their weakness," he says. "All they care about is winning."

"Some weakness."

"We stick together," he says. "We're family."

"If you're a family, why the hell do you need me?" I'm walking away, thinking I moved out of my mom's house when I was sixteen and I don't give a crap about family stuff, when I look over and see the Wailea guys laughing. They could be laughing at anything but I figure they're laughing at me. Ernesto grabs my shoulder, and says, "Listen. Do this for me, just this once, and after the race if you want me to go back to San Francisco, I will."

The brown scum is floating on the water, the storm drain by the loading dock is pumping, and the Wailea guys are still laughing next to their fancy-ass truck, so I hold out my hand to Ernesto and say, "Promise?"

We shake hands on it, and Ernesto leads me back to the Koa, where the local guys seem friendly, in a pre-gang-fight kind of way. After a couple of minutes listening to Ernesto and his friends say "We got to stay together. Together!" I'm all for dragging the canoe down to the beach, but Ernesto says, "It's koa." Which means we have to lift it onto our shoulders and carry it so the sand doesn't scrape the precious bottom. By the time we get it into the water, I'm hurting.

"Get in on the ama side," Ernesto says, like I don't know the basics. The water smells like paint thinner, and my feet sink in the mud while I make my way around behind Malama. Kawika sits in one, Ernesto behind him. They're the pace guys. Joey and Pancho, the two big guys, sit in the middle; they're the engine. I'm behind Pancho, in five. It's the best seat in the house because that's the widest part of the canoe and I got plenty of room. Behind me, in the steersman's seat, Malama is sucking on a cigarette.

Ernesto holds his paddle over his head with both hands, twists left and right, looks back at me. "Once we start," he says, "no one cept Malama talks."

"Yeah, sure." I don't expect much help from any of them.

"Hoe hapai," Malama says, almost in a whisper.

I wonder if Ernesto can hear her and I'm about to relay the message, whatever it means, when the rest of the gangee lift their paddles over their heads. I hold mine pointed at the water, Cali style, and Malama says, "Huki!"

I poke to the right, digging deep into the stinking harbor, and sure enough the ama pops out of the water. "Steady, gangee," Malama says. "Easy."

Yeah, yeah, it was my fault.

With me, Joey and Kawika paddling on the right, and Pancho and Ernesto on the left, the canoe moves through the water. Malama's steering so she has to fill in wherever she thinks best. A good steersman can make a boat go straight and get in a few good strokes. I'm not expecting much more than straight from Malama. We're going pretty good but the Wailea guys jump ahead like we're standing still, so I dig my paddle deep and pull as hard and fast as I can. The canoe jerks, glides, jerks, and Malama whispers, "Stay together, gangee. Stay together."

Twenty strokes on the right, then Joey calls, "Hut, hut, hut!" and we change sides, twenty strokes on the left. We cruise by the container ships, with the sun going down behind the mountains, and I start thinking that maybe we can give those fancy-ass bastards a race.

"Stay together, gangee," Malama whispers.

I slip back in rhythm.

"Hut, hut, hut!"

Point the blade at the water. Poke it deep. Pull. Lift. Poke. Pull. It feels good to pull in rhythm. Wailea is stronger than us, but they swing out a little too far and have to beat their way back against the surge to meet us at the harbor mouth. Malama glides us right along the edge of the smooth water behind the breakwater, so we're sitting there, resting, while they fight to get into position. Malama hands me the plastic bailer and I scoop out the water in the bottom of the canoe. By the looks of the ocean, there's going to be plenty more when we get outside the harbor. Over Pancho's shoulder, I see waves breaking all along Waihee Reef. The sun is setting behind the mountains. The navigation buoy is hidden behind rolling swells of dark water.

"What do you think?" the steersman from Wailea yells at us. I'm still scooping. We sit gently rocking on swells. I think the Coast Guard station is on the other side of the island, that we're crazy to go outside the harbor, but just as I'm about to open my mouth, Kawika raises his paddle over his head, and the rest of the gangee do the same.

"Ready," says the steersman from Wailea, and the fancy asses lean forward with their blades pointed at the water.

I look up at the sky. A rain drop hits me square in the forehead. I wait for more, but the clouds just hang there, black and ugly.

"Geeve 'em," Malama whispers, and I hear her cigarette hiss in the water. Quite an athlete, that Malama. Off we go, me digging like crazy because Wailea is already pulling ahead of us, the bailer bouncing around at my feet. As soon as we pass the breakwater, a huge swell hits us. The bow jumps in the air, and I'm looking up at Ernesto, his paddle digging in the air, then Ernesto goes down as I go up, and I'm looking down at Ernesto, my paddle digging in the air.

"Stay together, gangee," Malama whispers as the stern slams down. The shock hits me, then we're paddling in a trough between two swells, water splashing everywhere, and Ernesto shouts "Hut!"

I take one more stroke on my right, lift my paddle, the canoe wobbles, I switch to the left, dig the paddle in the water. Malama steers us straight for the buoy, straight into the swell.

"Stay together, gangee."

Sweat mixed with saltwater drips in my eyes.

"Stay together, gangee."

Wailea is off to our left, the surf pushing them toward the reef but they're so god-damned strong they're pulling ahead of us. A waves breaks across their bow, and their number-five drops his paddle and starts bailing with a plastic bucket.

"Stay together, gangee." It's like Malama is singing, a whisper-shouting kind of song.

Wailea's ama pops out of the water. Their number-four paddler leans out, grabs the outrigger, pushes it down. In a bright yellow flash, they smash through a wave. The whitewater pushes them back, turns them sideways. Their steersmen is yelling but I can't hear what. Their paddles jab at the water, digging them toward the darkness on the horizon.

"Feel the mana" Malama says. "Feel the mana."

When she digs her paddle I can feel the old canoe reach forward. For a skinny smoker girl, she knows the ocean. She's guiding us up and down waves in a straight line, keeping the bow pointed at the navigation buoy.

"Stay together."

We break through a wave. Water splashes over all of us, makes a river in the bottom of the canoe. The ama slaps at the sea. The gangee bend their backs, strain against the sea.

"Stay together, feel the mana."

We're actually pulling ahead of Wailea, and I'm thinking we're kicking ass, so I'm digging my paddle extra deep and extra hard, when the wave hits. Kawika and Eddie disappear in a wall of whitewater. Cold water wraps around me.

"Bailer," Malama shouts.

I'm jamming my paddle into the bottom of the canoe, reaching for the bailer, feeling for it through the foamy water, when the second wave hits and the canoe leans left. The next thing I know I'm knocked out, underwater, sinking. I must be crazy because I can still hear Malama whispering, "Stay together!"

When I kick to the surface, I'm looking at the beach, what there is of it. Between me and that jagged stretch of rocks and cliffs are three or four hundred yards of surf and coral reef. A swell about to break lifts me up, and I turn to see Wailea's canoe disappearing toward the horizon. Where's the Koa? I'm looking all over, freaking, when I see it about fifty yards away, down in a trough between two waves. Then it's gone, and I'm sliding down the back of the swell. A few second later, I'm back up again. Malama is cranking a left turn, digging hard to get the boat around before the next wave hits. With only four guys paddling it's an iffy proposition, putting the Koa broadside to the waves, but she's doing it.

To help, I bury my head in the water and stroke against the surf, trying to get as far away from the reef as I can. "Feel the mana," I hear her say underwater. "Feel the mana."

5. the language of nicotine

gina reached for a cigarette. Told herself no, da Professor hat-ed cigarettes. The last thing she needed was a lecture about smoking. She scratched her cheek, rubbed her nose, glanced at the newspaper editorial taped to the window. "Gap grows be-tween rich and poor on Big Island." Why did the Professor need so much stuffs on his window?

She found the conference list stuck between a train schedule for Europe and a black-and-white photograph of a sumo wres-tler. Her name was penciled in underneath Antonia Manlapit's. No telling how long da Professor would talk to dat girl. Gina peeked under the sumo wrestler's legs and saw the Professor sitting with his back to the window. Was he talking to his com-puter?

∞

The Professor whispered, "If you messing with one local woman," then repeated each word he had typed, "I am going to kill you." The police had told him to write down the caller exactly. What did that mean? Write down the caller? Three years now he had been living in Hilo, and no matter how hard he tried, writing pidgin was damned near impossible. The words never looked like they sounded coming from his students' mouths. Using two fingers, he typed, If you fuckin widt one local wahine, I goin keel yah. Was that exact enough?

When the phone rang, he spun in his chair, thankful that technology would soon replace the need to write. He pushed the answering-machine volume to maximum and leaned back, gazing out the window. The palms waved gently in the breeze. The clouds moved slowly across a blue sky. Two eyes peered at him from underneath a sumo wrestler's thick legs. Was she one of his students? He tilted his head. Angela? Or was it Gina? He had a hard time remembering their names, especially when they appeared as fragments, floating heads, trapped between the cultures on his window. He could use her face in a story he was writing, a postcolonial story, filled with melancholy, lost hope, and beautiful scenery. "Wait a minute," he called to her, thankful he had locked the door. Had he locked the door?

∞

Gina stepped back from the window. For a moment, she had felt the Professor inside her head, scratching around in there with his red pen. She sat down on the bench in the shade and spread her spiral notebook open on her lap. Her pencil felt too small for her swollen fingers. GOING BACKWARD? She wrote in ragged block letters. CAN THAT HAPPEN? CAN ONE PERSON MAKE YOU INTO A KID? MESS UP TIME?

∞

Inside the office, the answering machine clicked then recorded a garbled message. "Hel... Profes... Gr...stone. This is Profes... Chatterton... Basically, I... like ... talk ... your semester grades." The Professor reached for the phone but stopped himself by hoping that leaving message would satisfy her, like it might for the demented boyfriend. "Basically," she shouted, "you pass...we hurt the students ... not ready. You ... supposed to be in ... your office." Click.

The Professor looked forward to her arrival. And she would arrive, there was no way to stop her. He would enjoy telling Professor Chatterton that her new cell phone made her sound like she was speaking pidgin, electronic pidgin. It was not writing her down exactly. The Professor picked up a stack of writing exams. He was supposed to fail every student who could not write, in one hour and thirty minutes, an essay with fewer than three major grammatical errors. Standards had to be met. He thumbed through his stack of essays, counting quickly and looking at the names. Five fails, twenty passes. The last one belonged to a woman named Gina. It was riddled with red marks identifying major errors. At the top of the paper he had written C-. "No maddah how hard I try," he said, "I no can get it." He stood up and glanced out the window. Yes, she was Gina. He recognized the odd way she held her pencil, as if she were trying to crush it. She was sitting in the shade, notebook ready, but instead of writing, she was staring at the parking lot. That must be her problem. Easily distracted. It wouldn't hurt her to take the class again. Besides. She was old school, from a time when students didn't complain about teachers.

∞

Gina squeezed her pencil as she watched a red Honda Civic slide into the handicapped parking space next to the dumpster. The passenger, a thin woman in a brown skirt and clean white blouse, managed to squeeze out sideways, being very careful not to let the car door touch the dumpster. The driver yelled, "Hey, give me your cell."

Remembering bits and pieces of the Professor's lecture on specified details, Gina wrote quickly. ANTONIA MANLAPIT IS ONE CLEAN AND NEAT AND NICE GIRL, NOT LIKE THE ONES WHO WEAR TIGHT PANTS THAT BARELY COVER THEIR ...STUFFS. SHE IS WEARING OFFICE CLOTHES WITH BLACK AIR PULLED BACK.

Gina stopped writing long enough to watch Antonia lean in and kiss the driver. He slipped the cell phone from her hands as Gina tried quotation marks.

HE IS MEAN, I KNOW, BECAUSE HE NO CAN WAIT. ONE DAY HE MAKE HER GO AHEAD OF ME AND USE THE PRO- FESSOR'S TIME, AND THEN I STAY FOLLOWING PROFESSOR IN THE HALL BEGGING HIM TO LOOK AT MY ESSAYS, UNTIL THE PROFFESOR TOLD ME, "GINA, QUICK, OKAY, A SE- COND." PEOPLE STAY BRUSHING AGAINST ME, LOOKING AT ME, AND HE STAY POINTING OUT MAJOR ERRORS.

In the moment it took Gina to slap her notebook shut and stand up, she imagined thick nicotine smoke rushing down her throat, filling her lungs, driving out the scared feeling, for sure making her stomach go quiet. She needed to talk to the Profes- sor, but what if he corrected her subject-verbs, made her go back and start over before she got to the important part? Anto- nia was still kissing the boy. Gina stepped across the grass to the Professor's office. "Enough already," she said and twisted the doorknob, pushed.

The Professor glanced up from a stack of papers. "Oh," he said. "Gina, is it? Isn't Antonia first?"

Gina sat down and adjusted her purse in her lap. "You get one nice office," she said, choosing her words carefully. As long as he listened and didn't stop to correct her, she would be happy. "You read all doze books?" she asked

"What?"

"Doze books?" she said, nodding at the packed shelves.

"Doze" he said, scribbling the word on a UHPA note pad. I can use that.

She read the metal identification tab on the wood desk. Property of the Territory of Hawaii. The territory was a long time ago. Had people been coming to see English teachers that long? "Professor, I get one problem."

"You have a problem."

"Yes," she nodded. "I get one job."

"You have a job." The Professor was trying to correct her. Why didn't she understand? If only she could read the story he was writing, she would understand how difficult it was to do his job. The hero was a middle-aged Professor from the Mainland who falls in love with a Hawaiian girl named Haunani and helps her to save her mother's land from real estate developers. The Professor looked at Gina. Was she Hawaiian? He noted the wrinkles, the darkness under her eyes. How tired and old she looked. What was she doing back in school at her age?

Gina felt the bulge of cigarettes in her purse. "This morning I work seven hours after last night til one," she said. "Cleaning buildings, janitorial. I go back this afternoon."

"A difficult life," he said, wanting to correct her verb tense. While she talked, he glanced at her essay, coffee stained and smelling of cigarettes. She had chosen to write about the effects of unemployment on the Big Island. The introduction caught his attention. "My hands ache," she had written, "and in the morning I do not want to open my eyes." Two sentences later, however, she was off track, writing about how she had moved to the mainland as a teenager, been born and raised in Honolulu, married a military guy, one nut case, moved to the Mainland, got divorced, and moved to Paradise Park with a daughter to raise, alone, by herself. She wanted to make life better for her daughter. Now her daughter was divorced, with a kid and no job, and living at home.

Gina had stopped talking and was staring at the professor. "What should I do?" she said. "Can you help me?"

The air-conditioner recycled stale air while the Professor smiled to let her know he had been listening. What had she said? Her essay had made him feel like he knew her, in a Joycean stream-of-consciousness sort of way, but writing like Joyce wouldn't help her pass English 22. Standards had to be met. What if she ended up in the Department Chair's English 100 class? Sooner or later the Chair would ask her how she had managed to pass English 22. "Maybe," he said, "we should start with grammar. Each sentence has to be grammatically correct or the reader won't understand."

"I like write, Mister," Gina said. Her fingers, swollen, red at the knuckles, touched the edge of the paper, and the Professor was thinking that his story would have to end tragically. Maybe the Hawaiian woman would die of cancer.

"I no can afford to take English 22 again," Gina said.

The door swung open, and the Department Chair stepped into the room. "Excuse me. John, may I speak with you?" Before the Professor could answer, the Chair had retreated outside.

"Just a moment, Gina. I have to talk to Nurse Ratchet," the Professor said, proud of his literary allusion. As he stepped by her, he smelled cleanser and mildew. "From One Flew Over the Cuckoo's Nest," he said. "A literary allusion."

"One illusion," Gina said.

Closing the door behind him, the Professor wondered how he could use Gina's response in his story. The two lovers shared no cultural references, only the need for each other. How could their love survive the loss of allusions? He tried the sentence another way: How could their love survive the loss of illusions? Was there a way to make it funny and sad at the same time?

Gina closed her eyes and let the air-conditioner blow gently across her face. How nice it would be to work in an office like the Professor's. To have people come to her for help. When the phone rang, she grabbed her purse. When it rang again, she wanted to pick it up, to do the Professor a favor. He was still talking outside. The answering machine clicked and a man's voice shouted: "You fucking haole, I am going to kill you. You understand me now?" In the background, a woman's voice, a familiar voice, shouted, "Don't. Please!"

The machine clicked off.

Gina saw bits and pieces of the two professors talking. She opened the door and looked toward the parking lot. The boy, still sitting the driver's seat, tossed the cell phone into the parking lot and grabbed Antonia's arm, jerked her toward the car. The two professors were talking. Why couldn't they see what was happening? As Gina brushed by them, she heard the woman professor say, "If your student is too busy, she should try English when she has more time."

Gina had not run in years but she was running now, wishing she had a cigarette. The walkway stretched for miles. Gina wished he had a cigarette. The nicotine would give he stamina.

The boy was shaking Antonia.

"You stop dat!" Gina yelled. "You stop dat!"

"It's okay," Antonia was crying. "It's okay."

"Shame on you," Gina yelled, her slippers flip-flopping, slip-slapping on the concrete. It was happening again. Instead of the professor, this boy was in her head, making her go back in time, making her chase her daughter's car down the cinder driveway, feeling lost and helpless, trying to save her from what she knew was going to happen but could do nothing to change.

"Don't you go," Gina yelled, as Antonia ran around to the other side of the car and jumped in. The engine started, the boy flipped his finger at Gina. "Buggah," Gina said, reaching for the door handle. The car screeched backward, twisted, turned, and then raced down the hill, with Antonia slumped in the passenger seat.

Gina exhaled deeply, dug in her purse. She found her lighter and cigarettes, tapped out a USA special, lit the end, drew in a deep breath. The nicotine entered her lungs, filled them with soft clouds. She heard doors opening, students shuffling into the parking lot.

They brushed against her, talking about geology tests, semester grades, trips home to the mainland, to the Philippines, to Japan. Talking like haoles on MTV, like Japanese, Chinese, like locals. Talking Pidgin. Talking English. Standard English. All kines English. She closed her eyes and let their voices surround her, like smoke thick enough to inhale.

She wanted to remember the details, to be able to describe the boy if anything happened to Antonia. She told herself to write it all down. The crowd of students carried her along with them, and for a moment she was adrift in a wonderful spinning world of little girls and boys running from the school bus on the last day of school.

When she opened her eyes, she was back where she had started, standing in front of the Professor's office, looking at a newspaper headline. "Gap grows between rich and poor."

She inhaled, held the smoke inside. The world moved slower. It all made sense. Nicotine sense. She exhaled. The two professors were gone, and the office was empty, like an empty promise. She inhaled. That's a good one, she told herself. Like an empty promise. A simile, the Professor would call it. She pressed her finger against the glass, dragged it down the train schedule for Europe. Paris. Amsterdam, Berlin, Rome. To take the train she had to get the grammar right. Like an empty allusion. Life in a cuckoo's nest.

She exhaled. Inhaled. Big healthy sumo breaths.

With the cigarette dangling from her mouth, she took her favorite black pencil from her purse and wrote three lines across the sumo wrestler's stomach:

GINA STAY HERE.
2005.
I LIKE WRITE.

6. dreams of real estate

We were running in the sugarcane. Malama had a gun in her

hand, her father's .45, the one he had used to kill Japanese in the war, and I was dragging an empty duffel bag. We were trying to catch a bus

The cane was thick as water. Malama shoved it out of her way, smashed it flat. "Mana," she said over her shoulder. "It's strong here." Her face was hidden under a lau hala hat, reflector sunglasses and black moustache; her wonderful body covered by white polyester pants and a red aloha shirt plastered with pineapples. "Here," she said, kneeling and slipping her hand between stalks of fallen cane. "I feel it."

I felt sweat dripping from the Dolly Parton wig that was making my head itch. The gym socks stuffed in my bra were stretching my red flannel shirt almost to popping. My blue jeans were torn at the knee, and the cowboy boots I had borrowed were pinching my toes. My name is Johnny, but my friends call me

Friday because I go to church every Friday. Any church will do, as long as it's empty. An empty church is a nice place to sit and think about bills I have to pay, maybe drink a lite beer.

That morning in the cane I was disguised as Rita, a cowgirl from Makawao. Malama was supposed to be a tour guide named Kimo. The disguises were my idea. I didn't believe they'd fool anybody but I figured they'd confuse the issue. Malama had wanted to go as herself. She didn't care who recognized her. She only cared about her chance to stand in front of the Japanese and say, "Ua mau ke ea o ka ʻaina i ka pono." That's the Hawaii state motto. The official translation is "The life of the land is perpetuated in righteousness." Kamehameha III said it 1843. He was the third king of the unified Hawaii, the son of Liholiho and the grandson of Kamehameha the Great. He said it on the steps of Kawaiahaʻo Church after the British, who five months earlier had used a battleship to force him to cede Hawaii to their rule, saw the error of their ways and returned the islands to his hands. Malama knew all about Kamehameha III and the rest of Hawaii's history. She had a bachelor's degree in history from the University of California at Berkeley and a master's degree from the University of Hawaii. She was mostly Filipina but she was part Hawaiian too. She had this idea that Hawaii had been dying ever since 1778, when outsiders had first come to the islands and started stealing. Now the thieves were the Japanese. They were buying every inch of land, but to Malama the land was sacred. It couldn't be bought or sold.

I'd like to buy a home some day, a little acre somewhere for me and Malama. But it ain't going to happen. I licked thick red lipstick and said, "I don't feel nothing."

She grabbed my hand and pulled me through the cane. She was shorter than me but stronger. Maybe because she drew her power, her mana, from the earth and I drew mine from eggs and Spam. Her glasses were better, too. Hers looked like aviator/cop glasses. Mine had red lenses. They were heart shaped and too small for my head.

A blast of sunlight surrounded Malama as she pushed through the cane. "Time," she said. I stood still, afraid to move. The cane protected me from the outside world. Cars rushed by. Malama waved me forward with the gun. "The bus," she said.

I followed her as I knew I would. The sun was high in the sky, melting two lanes of black asphalt. A huge cane-haul truck rushed by and wind hit me in the face. Red dust and black exhaust settled like fallout from a nuclear explosion. "There," Malama said, pointing up the volcano. A silver and red bus rounded a curve. The Japanese were on the bus, tourists coming down from the volcano after taking pictures of the sunrise. It's very beautiful, the sunrise from Haleakala. I saw it once with Malama. That morning, dark and cold, had suddenly exploded bright orange. Malama said she couldn't breathe and I said that was because the top of the volcano was ten thousand feet high and she wasn't used to rarefied air. She said it was because gods lived at the top of Haleakala. Malama was a great believer in gods.

She poked me in the knee with the gun. "Ketchup," she said. I took a restaurant packet from my pocket and ripped it open with my teeth, squeezed ketchup on my knee. After I spread it around, I wanted to throw the empty container in the cane but Malama pointed the gun at me and said, "Respect for the land." So I stuffed the sticky plastic in my pocket. I wasn't afraid of the gun. It was empty. Bullets cost twenty dollars for a box at Maui Sporting Goods, and we figured fifty cents apiece was too much for bullets we'd never use. We didn't want to hurt anybody. I only wanted to help Malama, and she only wanted to turn back the tide. That's all.

"My father fought the Japanese," Malama said. She took a deep breath, held it as if she were smoking. "They tried to kill him."

"Not these Japanese."

"Some of them. The war wasn't that long ago. Some of them are still alive."

The bus slowed down on another curve.

"I don't hate them," Malama said. "They're people like us, but they have too much money. They're drowning us in their money. They're the new white man."

She had told me all this before, but I figured she needed to say it again because it's a big jump from waitress to hijacker, even in dreams.

Why she likes me, I don't know, except that the first time she saw me, I was walking out of church. It was a Friday, and she's a great believer in signs from the gods. That was when she was working for the planning commission, before she threw the councilman's files in the street.

"We have to stop them," she said. "We have to save Maui, not sell it to the highest bidder."

"A man's got to do what a man's got to do," I said, wiping lipstick off the corner of my mouth. It was hot and still.

"When they hear my tape, they'll understand," Malama said. She was crouched down, gun in hand, ready. I kicked a spider off my cowboy boot. "I've never stolen anything," I said.

"Don't lie."

"A dollar from my mom's purse, once. Maybe twice. And when I was an altar boy I took five dollars from the collection plate, but I've never pointed a gun at anybody."

She looked at the gun, squeezed it until her fingers turned white. "I have to do it," she said. "No one will listen to me." The wind blew across the tops of the cane.

"Keep them in their seats," she said. "And don't let them take pictures. All Japanese have cameras." She was practicing her man's voice. It sounded convincing, more convincing than my woman's voice. Malama had more acting experience than me. She played Hamlet in her senior class play, I played a shepherd in my third-grade Christmas play. "Be in charge," she said. "Command."

I wiped sweat from my nose. Adjusted the socks in my bra. "You know what cured me of stealing?" I said.

"And don't let them take videos."

"When I was living in Lahaina, I didn't eat meat for a year, to save enough money for a bike. I bought a ten-speed. The second day I had it, someone stole it. I haven't stolen anything since."

Malama grabbed my arm, shook me. "The money doesn't mean anything. We have to show them we're serious. When the tourists stop coming, they'll stop building hotels. They're stealing our souls. How else can we make them stop? Take out an ad in the newspaper? Vote for our councilman?"

In her sunglasses I saw my reflection: a blonde wearing heart-shaped sunglasses.

"The Japanese have more money than they can use," she said.

"We're doing them a favor."

"We can't touch the politicians, the CEOs, the real estate developers, but right here, right now, we can get the tourists!"

"Strike a blow," I said, adjusting my falsies.

She led me to the middle of the road. I was leaning on her shoulder, my arm wrapped around her neck. The bus, silver and red, brakes and engine noise, rolled toward us. "Be strong," she said.

The bus had a rainbow painted between its headlights. It looked like an upside down smile.

We stood our ground. A big guy was driving. He was getting bigger. He had two chins: a regular one and a big fat one. He was smiling, yellow teeth flashing, as if he were going to enjoy smashing us into the asphalt.

"Jump," I yelled.

Malama stood her ground.

The bus screeched, skidded to a stop an inch from my nose. I saw brush strokes in the rainbow's red paint, thought of praying to one of Malama's gods, but didn't know any by name. "Mana," I whispered.

We hobbled to the door. Malama banged on glass, but the driver shook his head, he was leaning over, giving us a close look. I kept my head down and rubbed my knee. "She's hurt," Malama said. "Please."

The driver's mouth formed the words COM-PA-NY PO-LI-CY and he settled back in his seat, looked at the road, ready to leave us, but a Japanese woman with a big yellow hibiscus flower pinned to her chest tapped him on the shoulder and said something, pointed at us. He shook his head. The woman dug into him. She pointed, tapped his shoulder. Like me, I guess the driver knew there was no hope arguing, because he pushed a button and the door popped open with a whoosh of crisp cold air that hit me in the face, as he said, "It's your responsibility, lady."

Malama climbed in and pointed the .45 at his nose. "The life of the land is in me," she said.

I pulled myself up the steps. The air smelled of after-shave and expensive perfume. The driver had a nametag: Al. Al wasn't happy to see us. When Malama pointed the gun at him, he closed his eyes and said, "I' told you they were hippies!"

"Drive," Malama said. The door shut. The bus lurched forward.

A hundred Japanese looked at me. They were old, young, thin, fat, angular, round. A few of them were wearing glasses. All of them were wearing yellow baseball caps with pink lettering that said HERE TODAY, GONE TO MAUI.

"What now?" Al said.

"Drive slow," Malama said. "Don't try anything funny. Stop when you get to Hana Highway. Light or no light."

A taped voice was yakking in Japanese, probably about cane fields and how Maui's central valley was the largest sugar producing area in Hawaii. Malama said, "Kill the tape."

Al pressed a button and the tape died. The hum of air-conditioning took its place.

Malama pointed the gun at the back of the bus and said, "Ua mau ke ea o ka aina i ka pono." The Japanese looked at each other. The woman with the hibiscus was sitting behind Al. She touched Malama's elbow gently, with a tiny finger, and pointed at her nametag, half hidden under hibiscus. Her nametag had something written in Japanese and below that: Miss Takamori. "I am a translator," she said. "I am sorry, I do not speak Hawaiian."

"The language of the people," Malama said. "It means the life force continues in nature now that things are properly ordered. Tell them."

Miss Takamori turned to the Japanese and gave them the news. The Japanese nodded politely.

"Ua mau ke ea o ka aina i ka pono!" Malama said.

Miss Takamori rattled off the translation. A couple of Japanese fiddled with cameras.

"No pictures," I said in a squeaky voice. Everyone looked at me as if they were expecting further instructions. "No videos."

Miss Takamori translated.

"Stay in your seats and throw your wallets and purses in the duffel bag," Malama said.

Miss Takamori translated.

I held the bag up for them to see, shook it, and noticed Antonio Manlapit stenciled in faded black ink near the top of the bag. Antonio Manlapit was Mr. Manlapit, Malama's father. I was rolling the top of the bag down so his name would disappear when Al tried something funny by swerving the bus into the other lane.

I landed in an old woman's lap. She was small and brittle, with thick glasses, wrinkles, and a mole on her cheek. The wind rushed out of her. Malama pointed the gun at Al's head and the bus swerved back into the right lane. I stood up in a hurry. "Sorry," I said and held the bag open. The old guy next to her was holding her hand, They were a cute couple, in an old-sorta way. She dropped a black purse in the bag, and he dug in his back pocket, found a faded brown wallet, and dropped it in Mr. Manalapit's bag.

"Thank you," I said. I didn't like taking their money. Old people need money, and whenever I look at old Japanese people I think of atom bombs. I don't feel guilty but I figure that anybody who has memories like that deserves a friggin peaceful bus ride on vacation.

Malama was talking to Al, shaking her tape in front of his face. I slipped the purse out of the bag and gave it to the old lady.

"Ua mau ke ea o ka aina i ka pono!" said Malama's voice on tape. "Turn it up," her real voice said. The volume went up.

I turned my attention to the man and woman across the aisle. They were young. She was wearing bright clingy clothes, pink and yellow, and he looked like a Harvard man, with tortoiseshell glasses, a pink polo shirt and green pants. He was smirking, like he could care less. He tossed his alligator wallet, gold watch and cigarette lighter into the duffel bag. His babe used two fingers to drop in a pink purse. Them, I didn't mind robbing. I liked the chrome Zippo, the kind my dad had used in the war.

Cars were whizzing past us, heading up the mountain, and Malama's tape was talking up a storm, explaining how the first Hawaiians had sailed from the Marquesas in 300 A.D. and crossed more than two thousands miles of ocean without maps or charts. Five hundred years later the Tahitians arrived. Then mysteriously the migrations stopped and the Hawaiian civilization developed for a thousand years without contact from the outside world. Then came Captain Cook.

Malama stopped the tape so Miss Takamori could translate. I kept moving up the aisle. The bag was getting so big and fat I could hardly move. The Japanese were throwing in cameras, radios, purses, wallets and box lunches. The bus seemed to be going faster, the cane fields were a blur.

Malama's tape blabbed on about King Kalaniopuu killing Captain Cook in 1779 and how for seven years the white sailors avoided the islands but not even the memory of the famous navigator's death could overpower their greed, keep them from returning. The whaling fleets needed the islands to provision their ships and merchants wanted to trade for the rich supply of Hawaiian rosewood that could be sold in China. With the help of Ku, the war god, King Kamehameha unified the islands under his rule and held back the foreigners, but when Kamehameha died, the missionaries came.

I reached the back of the bus and looked out the rear window. The road was a long black empty strip. We were going so fast, cars couldn't stay up with us. When I turned around, Malama was yelling at Al. "Slow down. NOW!"

Through the front window I saw the Hana Highway intersection. There wasn't going to be time for any more history lessons. Malama shouted: "Our land was stolen from us!"

Miss Takamori translated. I shoved the bag down the aisle. I didn't look at the Japanese, I didn't want to see any more of their faces. Instead, I looked at my reflection in the window. I had this stupid smile on my face, a nasty grin from trying to be friendly and mean at the same time, with lipstick on my teeth. The Japanese didn't say anything. Maybe they were too embarrassed.

Malama was shouting over the tape, "This land belongs to Hawaiians. The people who are selling it to the Japanese have no right to sell it. Go back to Japan and tell your people not to come here. Tell them the roads are dangerous. Tell them their buses will be hijacked. Do you understand?"

Miss Takamori spelled it out for them. She spoke quickly, clearly. For all I knew she was giving them instruction on how to get to the buffet. The Japanese nodded their heads. My arms were hurting by the time I squeezed by Malama. The bag weighed a ton. The bus was going ninety miles an hour.

"Stop," Malama yelled.

Al kept his foot on the gas until Malama buried the gun barrel between his chins. He hit the brakes. The bus bumped and hopped and skidded on the gravel shoulder. I fell down the stairs, slammed into the door. The young guy, Mr. Harvard with the tortoise-shell glasses, lunged for Malama, but she had her knees bent, surfer style, one hand braced against the dash, and she was quick. Before he could get a hand on her, she pointed the gun at his rich-guy face. "Get back."

He understood without Miss Takamori having to translate.

Al hit the brakes again and we skidded to a stop a couple of feet from the cane. Mr. Harvard stared at me. His girlfriend was crying and the old lady across the aisle was looking at the floor. We were all very serious.

"Open the door," Malama said.

Al didn't move. "If I were a gambling man," he said, "I'd bet you aren't man enough to use that gun."

That made me laugh but Malama didn't take it so good. She stuffed the gun barrel between his chins. "Man enough!" she said. "Man enough!"

The door popped open and the heat hit me like a heavy-weight. I kicked the duffel bag onto the gravel. A red pickup truck rushed past, shot through the intersection, heading for the ocean, the driver leaning out the window, looking back at me. The wind was blowing through the cane but I couldn't hear it over the clatter of the bus engine. I love the sound of wind in the cane. It always reminds me of waves breaking.

"You have to understand," Malama yelled into the bus as she backed down the steps. "We're dying."

"That's right," I said, dragging the bag over gravel.

Miss Takamori kept translating. I had a feeling she was like us. The hibiscus gave her away. People who hide their nametags have a wild streak. The old couple was leaning toward Al, checking if he was okay.

"I don't feel so good," I said.

Malama pulled me toward the cane. The bag fell out of my hands. Wallets and purses spilled onto the side of the road. Al snapped the door shut. We were standing alone, Malama straight and tall, one hand holding a gun, the other balled into a fist, me bent over, my hands on my knees, feeling kinda seasick. "I don't feel right."

"Leave the bag," she said.

"The costumes were a bad idea," I said. "I can't be a revolutionary in a blonde wig."

There was a tear on her cheek.

"I'd rather rob a bank than a bus," I said, "A bank is just vaults and money." The old couple had screwed us. I can't go around doing stuff like this to old people. "A bus is too personal. Next time we should rob a bank, but not a credit union."

"They understood," Malama said, and disappeared into the cane.

I grabbed the duffel bag, turned it upside down. The rest of the wallets, purses, and cameras tumbled onto the gravel. I found the chrome Zippo under a DKNY bag. I held it up so Mr. Harvard could see and then dropped it in my bra. As I slipped into the cane, I looked back at the bus. The Japanese had opened their windows and were leaning out, clapping. Maybe they thought we were a show put on by a tour company. Or maybe Malama was right. Maybe they understood. They were clapping so loud I heard them five minutes later, deep in the cane, me sitting in Mr. Manlapit's old jeep, Malama driving, red dust flying everywhere.

She had thrown away her hat and sunglasses. The moustache was still stuck to her lip, and she was laughing, her face alive with sunlight. I ripped off my sunglasses and the world exploded in blues and greens. "Can you feel it?" she said, gripping the steering wheel as we crashed through the cane. I felt bumps and dips, and cane slapping me in the face. I felt the Zippo slip out of my bra and land on my belly button. The old jeep was shaking itself to pieces.

7. high test blues

---

talk about a scary love story.

Friday night, I'm in Honolulu for the weekend, sipping high test at Gordon Biersch when this angelica drops out of the sky. "Please," she says, her delicate finger tapping the empty chair, "can you help me?"

Like, it's a question?

I mean, she's Jade Moon with Patricia Ford's body squeezed into an ethernet dress delicately scented with opium perfume. "This may sound crazy," she says, her x-ray eyes burning a hole in my heart, "but I'm looking for a man."

Me, suddenly, I'm the naked guy in a Calvin Klien ad, you know, attractive. When Bam! Faster than you can say pau hana six pack, two huge guys, as big as Tongans only bigger, bust out of Sloppy Joe's, strangling each other and crashing into tourists. And right behind them explodes this comet-trail of drunken aloha shirts and screeching Hooters girls. Waiters are shouting,

---

cops are pointing. Everything is flying everywhere. Tables, glasses, garlic fries, Jell-O shooters, push-up bras. It's so damned wacky, any second I'm expecting Quentin Tarentino to pop out of a brewery vat and scream, "Action! Shoot somebody!"

Anyways, I'm sitting there all calm and collected trying to keep the angelica interested when this Hooters girl brunette from Punahou slams into the table and lands in my lap. It's like bonus Friday. "Man" she says, adjusting her t-shirt, "I can't believe what just happened."

Neither can I but I'm not complaining, even though she goes about 135, which is a load on your lap if you been drinking beer all afternoon.

"Him," she says, pointing at the two big guys fighting. "Stretch friggin' Langley!"

And sure enough, she's right. When the two big guys bounce off the bar, I see that one of them has a huge bicep wrapped around the other guy's head, and on that bicep is a tattoo of Isaac Newton. Isaac friggin' Newton.

Only guy in Hawaii who has that kind of tattoo has to be Stretch Langley. You remember him from the news? The guy from Kaimuki High School who went off his beaner? I knew him back in college. He was always lifting weights. I'd say to him, Stretch, let's go surfing, cruise the Rainbow Drive-in, find some girls, and he'd say, "Not me. I got something growing in me." Then he'd go back to lifting weights.

When he wasn't pumping iron, he was hearing voices, even back then. We'd be sitting at Aloha Stadium, watching the Bows get beat 45-6 by Mississippi Mid-tech, and in the middle of all the halftime show he'd drop his peanuts and say, "Did you hear that? Did you?" The only thing I could hear was 28,000 people snoring and the band playing the Hawaii 5-0 theme, but he'd smile and nod and say, "That's her. That's her."

Who the her was I never knew. I never saw him with a girl. He looked like a young Jason Scott Lee, and girls were always chasing him, but Stretch never had time for them. He was too busy lifting weights and listening to voices. Some days he'd lift for three or four hours. He lifted so much he got double huge. He got so big, the football coach at UH tried to get him a scholarship but Stretch said no, he didn't like football and he didn't like the new helmets. People got hurt playing football, that's what Stretch said. Remember, this is the guy who could bench press 450 pounds with both hands tied behind his back.

He must have kept lifting even after he got out of college, because the night I saw him trying to strangle the bouncer at Aloha Towers, he was still big enough to be the statue of Father Damien in front of the state building. You know, the one on steroids. The waitress from Hooters warming my lap was just about to tell me how the fight had started when Stretch and the guy he was strangling ricocheted off the bar, just missed a baby stroller, and bounced the Hooters girl out of my reach, then rolled to the edge of the dock. All the time, Stretch is yelling, "Where is she? Where is she?"

Then Bam! Everything freezes.

The crowd shuts up. Beers hang in midair. And Stretch and his partner are locked in a twisted 45-degree-angle double-headlock, hanging off the dock. For a second it gets so quiet the only thing I hear is my angelica's heart beating, which sounds like the pitter-patter of baby's feet on wet sand.

"Two high tests," I call to the waiter, figuring it's my only chance to beat the rush. (Heck, sometimes it's impossible to get a beer in the place on Friday night.) "Exports?" he says, playing dumb.

"High tests!" I shout. "Two of them."

Somehow, I don't how, the waiter manages to scoot around all the frozen-in-place people and hand the angelica and me two chilled glasses of the house's best brew. My first sip makes the gears catch, and everyone is moving again. Stretch slips free of the headlock. He ducks, he weaves. He shoves the bouncer in the chest. Frontal force out. The bouncer falls back, swinging his arms like he's trying to fly, slips, and drops over the edge, out of sight, screaming, "I can't swim. I can't."

You sure you don't remember Stretch? Even after he got his MBA, he didn't get much smarter. He worked construction down at BenCo for $10 an hour plus medical, Kaiser not HMSA, because he didn't want to compromise his principles by working Downtown with the uniform-aloha-shirt crowd. He thought he could jam his thick head in a hard hat and save enough money at $10 an hour to buy a condo in Kapolei. Yeah, right. His boss, Hero Silva, put him to work driving truckloads of dynamite or nitroglycerin or napalm, whatever it is they use to blast holes for highways, up into the mountains where they were building H3.

You remember what happened then, right? One day he gets up there in a muddy valley crawling with birds and bushes and waterfalls, and he's ready to set off an atomic blast, when all over again he starts with the voices. "I hear her," he says, hand poised on plunger. "I hear her."

Me, I would've told him to fire away, but Silva thinks Stretch is for real, so he calls in the state. And the state calls in the army, and the army calls in the navy, and the navy throws in the seals, and for three weeks, they thrash around up there in the waterfalls and green stuff, searching for lost hikers. But nobody finds anything except mosquitoes.

That's what they get for listening to a lolo like Stretch, right?

Anyway, back at Aloha Tower, Stretch throws the bouncer off the pier, and I hear Ka-splaassh. The next second the whole crowd is shadowed under a mushroom cloud of harbor sludge.

Oh, man, the smell is pure hell. Ever wonder what's at the bottom of Honolulu Harbor? Don't. So the mushroom cloud descends and everyone but the angelica gets soaked in stinky water. Angelica stays perfectly dry. It's a miracle, except for this tiny black drop of diesel-fuel-ocean water that settles on her cheek, like a tear.

I can't explain why, but seeing that tear and then the mob surging forward, building, swarming toward Stretch, who they figure is the cause of them being soaked in stink water, made my gut ache. And right then, I knew exactly how it felt to be in love. But I didn't have time to savor it, because the brunette from Punahou, the Hooters girl who had bounced out of my lap, was acting all snotty. You know how they do. Anyway, she's flippin and she screams, "Get him!"

Well, I think she means the bouncer, so I push through the crowd and I rip the rescue buoy off its rusty nail. You know me, once a lifeguard always a lifeguard. And I toss it down to the big guy flopping around like he doesn't know how to swim. He grabs the buoy and the last I see of him, he's kicking toward the Grigoriry Kozintsyev, a freighter from Russia that's full of sweltering, volatile fish meal.

But it turns out the waitresses from Punahou isn't worried about the bouncer. She wants Stretch. "Get him!" she screams again. And the mob lunges, and I think we're both going over the edge, but Stretch grabs me and my beer. "Find her," he says, ripping open his shirt and revealing six fat PVC pipes strapped to his chest and wired to a chess clock. "I don't want to hurt anybody." Which doesn't seem quite right if you ask me. If he didn't want to hurt anybody, why is fingering that clock and my neck? That's what I'm thinking, when the waitress yells, "He's bluffing!"

Talk about crazy. Does she know this is the Stretch Langley who strapped himself to the H3 tunnel and threatened to blow himself up unless they stopped work on that freeway? The guy it took five construction workers from Samoa to toss into the back of a dynamite truck so they could drive him to Queen's Medical? Does she know this is the Stretch that the doctors, trained professionals, diagnosed as so screwed up that they shipped him UPS Same-Day to Kaneohe Hospital and told the guys over there to lock him up for life.

Oh, now you remember him. Yeah, the slightly suicidal guy who kept hearing voices. And the only reason he got out of the hospital was Governor Ben closed the place to save money. Yeah, that Stretch. Him.

So he's fingering my neck and the chess clock, which I notice is the digital kind that costs $59.99. We make a pretty postcard. Diamond Head and two giant condo towers that look like electric bug zappers in the background. Aloha from Hawaii. Having a wonderful vacation. Wish you were here to see the explosion!

I'm breathing in my last breath, wondering what it will be like to be blown across town to Waikiki. When bam! up pops my angelica in her Ethernet dress. She fast, that babe, even in high heels. Right at Stretch she flies, trailing opium perfume. She tackles him around the chest, knocks me clear, and lifts him off his feet. For a second they're suspended over the water.

Then they drop. I look over the edge. The splash hits me like a bad dream. I stagger back waiting for the explosion. But nothing happens. Everything is quiet. They're gone. Never to be seen again

You think I'm lying? You don't believe me?

Listen, I jumped in and dove down into the harbor muck and looked for hours but I couldn't find anything. No Stretch. No angelica. Nothing. Just oily rags, fish heads, and an old chess clock.

But that's not the scary part.

Last Friday night, just before sunset, I'm sitting here drinking High Test. And I'm thinking about the price of beer, wondering if $5 is a lot to pay, when I hear a voice over by the water. It's a whisper. So I walk to the edge of the dock, and I hang my ear over, and sure enough, I recognize my angelica's voice. Believe me, I know that voice. And I hear Stretch, too, the two of them, down there in the dark ocean, moving, rolling, saying. "Love. Love. Love."

It's like a song with one word that's making me sleepy and dopey, and for a long second I want to jump down in that ocean and drown with them. The only thing that saves me is the bartender, when he yells, "Last call!"

That shakes me back to reality, because hearing voices is important but last call is something that shouldn't be ignored, no matter what. "Did you hear that?" I ask the bartender, and he says, "No. What'd you order? High Test?"

Now tell me, is that scary or what?

saturday

8. home run

---

a home run, a nice fat home run, that's what Matthew needed.

And he was going to nail one. A nice fat home run, smack dab over the right-field fence.

He knew, you didn't have to tell him, not him, that the game was only a stupid, no-nothing, excuse-to-drink joke in the Saturday-morning-county-softball league, where Matthew's team was buried so deep in last place they had to look up to see their slippahs. Hell, even if they won every game from here to eternity they'd still finish last. Matthew didn't care. He was going to hit a home run.

The night begged for it. In more ways than one, it was begging for it. First, there was the wind blowing off the ocean, whipping through the chicken-wire backstop and heading straight to right field, kicking up infield dirt along the way, before it knocked Fred Nishiki's red cap into the air. Second, there was Fred Nishiki, running all alone in right field, chasing his hat

---

toward the outfield fence. Old Fred Nishiki, fifty pounds too fat and slower than a county worker on Friday afternoon. Hell, he couldn't even catch his hat. One good swing of Matthew's bat, and Fred would be sinking in deep kim chee. And third, anyway, Fred wasn't going to get the chance to be a hero, because Matthew was going to hit a home run.

Matthew needed a home run to wipe five days of bullshit off da slate with one good swing of the bat. Just like that. Matthew smiled to himself. What a way to end the week, with a nice fat home run. Nothing could be finer, nothing, than a nice fat home run.

Matthew strutted to home plate, kicked his size-twelve Reebok at the red dirt, and then, and only then, after pulling his cap down and his pants up, he tapped home plate with his Kirby Puckett aluminum bat. A Cinderella story, that what he was. Just like in the movies. Bottom of the ninth. One man on. One man out. One run down. A home run would win the game. And because he deserved it, because the world contained a sense of justice, Matthew told himself, he was going to hit it, smash it, drive it over the fence. All week he had been a loser, the worst of the worst, a doormat. Not any more.

No more Joey Lassado chewing him out for being late. No Mrs. Rodrigues yelling at him for scraping the paint on her Toyota Tercel. No more Benny Tanaka, cooler-guard from hell, claiming he was cockroaching beer. No more nothing about paying off a bet on the Sonics. Hell, what did they know? All of them. Them!

Jesus, a few minutes late. One little scratch on a car. Two beers. A lousy fifteen bucks. And him, who says he didn't know about attitude and how to talk to customers!

Hell, he knew how to talk to customers. The boss didn't have to tell him nothing. He knew more about talking to loudmouth customers than the boss knew about talking to lousy loudmouth customers. Shoot. No matter. The week was behind him now. Now, it was his turn to be on top. Wait till Angie saw him knock one out. She'd fall all over him when they got home. Kiss the hero, just like back in the school days, when he was running the bases for Baldwin High. The Big Bear, that's what she had called him.

There she was now, sitting in the stands next to stinky Mary Medeiros, probably listening to her blab about soap operas. That's all women ever talked about--General Hospital, All My Children, the Young and the Senseless. And where the hell was his kid? Had she let him wander off to the hot dog stand? He didn't want his kid off eating a hot dog while he hit a home run. No, there he was sitting behind Stinky Mary, hiding behind her massive mountain of flesh. Why was that kid so shy? Hadn't he told him a hundred times, no, a thousand times, not to hide behind Stinky Mary. And what does the kid do? What? Hide behind Stinky Mary! That had to stop.

But right now Matthew had to forget about kids. He didn't care if everyone of them in the world hid behind Mary. That wasn't important right now. A home run, that was important.

Rudy Wilbur, the catcher, pulled his mask off his face and said, "Can we play now, Matthew? Are you ready?"

"Sure I'm ready."

"Sure, you're ready. Ready for another strikeout?" Rudy spit a wad of pink gum at Matthew's Reebok, and knelt in the dirt, jamming his fist into his fat mitt.

"Not this time," Matthew snapped, kicking the gum at Rudy and wishing the league allowed cleats.

Bill Hurts waved at him from the mound. "What? Three strikeouts not enough for you, Matthew?"

"I'm going to knock it right over your thick head." So what if he had struck out three times? So what? He had the best batting average on the team. He had the most hits, the most doubles, the most home runs. That's what counted. No one on the team was any better than him. That's what counted. Three strikeouts in one night didn't mean anything, except that he had been having a bad Saturday. No one would remember strikeouts after he hit a home run.

"Play ball," the umpire barked, then out of the side of his mouth said, "Not you again, Matthew. Haven't you had enough?"

Matthew spread his feet shoulder wide, dug his toes into the dirt, planted his heels, settled his weight on the balls of his feet, lifted the bat off his shoulder, shook it twice to throw off the pitcher, and finally, to please the fans, checked the first base coach for a sign. Down the line, Benny Kaiwi touched his finger to his nose. Bunt! Matthew screamed inside his head. He wants me to bunt! No way. The best hitter on the team. What does he mean, bunt? Not now, not never.

"Strike," yelled the ump.

"What? Hey, I didn't even see the ball."

"You saying I can't call a game?"

"I'm saying I wasn't ready."

"Not my fault."

Matthew stepped out of the batter's box and shook his shoulders loose. Old Fat Fred edged in from the fence, rubbing his bald head, moving closer and closer to the infield. Let him come, let him come. Matthew stepped to the plate.

Benny Kaiwi touched his finger to his nose.

"Ain't no way," Matthew spit, letting the next pitch sail high over his head. "No way."

"Ball one."

"That's right," Matthew pointed the fat end of the bat at the pitcher. "That's right."

"Shut up and get back in the box," Hurt yelled. "We can't wait around all night for you to swing. Didn't the boss already warn you about being late?"

Creep, Matthew said to himself, hugging the plate, daring Hurt to try and hit him. The bat felt light in his hands. Perfect. Just right, as if it were loaded with dynamite. He pictured the ball exploding over the right field fence.

Benny Kaiwi touched his finger to his nose.

"Forget it," Matthew grumbled. "Stick your finger in your nose for all I care."

The next pitch missed the plate by an inch.

"Ball two."

"That's right," Matthew said, checking to see if his wife was still watching. There she sat, biting down on a hot dog while the boy peeked over Mary's shoulder.

"Great," grumbled Matthew.

"Talking to yourself again?" the catcher said, flashing two fingers for a fastball.

"Not me," Matthew snapped.

Benny Kaiwi touched his finger to the his nose.

"I don't believe it. I'm the best hitter in the league. Why? Why? Why?"

"Who's the best hitter in the league?" the catcher spit into his mask.

"Quit squawking and play ball," the umpire snapped, and the next pitch sailed over the plate for ball three.

"Too high. Even a blind man could see that." Matthew rested the bat on his shoulder. Now he had it made. This was it. Three-and-one. One man out. The pitcher tossing big fat ones. Home run time. And what was even better, Old Fat Fred had waddled closer to the infield grass. Matthew charged up every muscle and stared at Benny Kaiwi, daring him to give him the sign.

Benny touched his finger to his nose.

I don't believe it. I don't believe it. Matthew kicked dirt at the catcher's feet, stomped his foot, shook his bat. Why is this happening to me?

"Watch where you kick that dirt, Matthew, or I'll kick you out of the game."

Hurt cranked his arm in a swirl of a circle and pitched a slow-pitch type blooper that sailed right down the middle, fluttered like a heavyweight butterfly, right where Matthew could see it. And for a second, for a split second, Matthew thought about swinging away, hitting the ball as hard and as far as he could. Then he thought of team loyalty and honor and doing the right thing, and so, at the last second, he dropped the end of his bat, a bit too fast, and tapped, whacked, almost bunted, but sort of pushed, the fat pitch onto the ground, right past the pitcher. Matthew clawed his way out of the batter's box, heaved himself toward first, as the ball hopped into the waiting hands of the short stop, who flipped it to second for one out, while Matthew sucked in huge gulps of air and pumped his arms, threw his knees high in the air, half man, half machine, a locomotive derailed, as the short stop leaped into the air, spun, threw, and Matthew dove, cursed, flew toward first, racing a looping throw that slapped into the first baseman's mitt, a second, an inch before Matthew crashed into the bag, face first.

"You're out!"

Matthew rolled over on his back and saw Old Fat Fred, his stomach leading the way, pass over him like a dark cloud. "Good try, Matthew!" Fred said. "Slowing down, aren't you."

"You idiot," Matthew grumbled at Benny Kaiwi.

"Who you calling an idiot."

"You. I'm calling you an idiot."

"You're the one eating dirt. Sliding into first. Whoever heard of anyone sliding into first?"

"I wouldn't be sliding into first if you knew your butt from a cement truck. Me. the best hitter on the team, and You gave me the bunt sign."

"What bunt sign?"

"Touching your nose, you suckah."

"That's the hit-away sign, I was telling you to knock one out.

Matt looked up at the sky, then at his tired feet. "Christ," he said, "Friggin Saturdays."

9. no outward sign

---

finally," Gina whispered. "Going home."

I wasn't so sure. Through the 300mm lens, I saw the twin-engine Otter, drop from the clouds, skid along the asphalt, and rush toward the narrow strip of sand that separated the runway from ocean. Its bird-of-paradise logo reminded me of a story I had written a few years back. A similar plane with the same logo had disappeared into one of Molokai's inaccessible valleys. No one had survived.

Click: Kalaupapa, a moment before disaster. In those days, I always took a shot of the plane I was about to fly in so I could leave it with the station people. If anything happened to me, at least someone would make a buck. It was sick, I know, but it made me feel like a professional.

The plane jerked to a stop, a body length from a hand-painted sign that warned, Go no further! Farther! No doubt written by the same confused state worker who had scribbled above the leaky toilet in the visitors' Quonset hut: Please giggle the handle!

Click: Ignored warnings.

"We don't need pictures of a plane," Gina said, swatting at the lens.

The paper had sent us out to get shots of Kalaupapa before the state replaced most of the old stuff with a National Historic Park. The isolated peninsula was crawling with state and federal employees. During the past two days, I'd shot doctors, administrators, carpenters, forest rangers, even a priest and nun, but no patients. There were supposed to be eighty-seven who had chosen to live out their lives on the peninsula. Where had they been hiding? A nice 8x10 would have made everyone happy.

I switched from the telephoto to a wide angle, the same 28mm that I had dropped through the rotted floor of the detention center two years ago on Angel Island. Now I used it frame the tiny open-air terminal on Kalaupapa. Click: Five university students heat-slumped in plastic chairs. Click: Four construction workers gulping beer from red and white cans dug from a plastic cooler. Click: One old woman hugging a pet's traveling cage to her chest.

I switched back to the 300mm for a close-up of the old woman. Character in the shape of wrinkles always sells. Click: Pale cheeks, age-spotted hands. Click: Pink sweatshirt stretched over a protruding belly. Click: Green double-knit slacks, baggy at the knees and ankles. Click: Swollen ankles bulging out of white shoes. The ordinary body of an all-too-ordinary old woman, probably a public health nurse or office worker on her way to Vegas for the weekend.

Gina hefted her canvas duffel bag onto her shoulder and stared at the thick white clouds hanging in the sky. Click A worried traveler: Click: A disgruntled journalist. Click: A young woman who likes to swim naked. "I can't believe this place," she said, shading her eyes with her hand. Click: In the background, a thin strip of Kalaupapa's rugged peninsula, a tiny splash of the

80

colony's blue harbor, and, beyond the water, towering above Gina, was the two-thousand-foot cliff that had held us prisoner. Click: No escape.

The pilot kicked the boarding ladder out of the plane and stepped carefully toward the concrete. The instant his foot touched ground, he waved us forward. Click: Waving to refugees.

By the time I had loaded a new roll of film, left the roll at the ticket counter, and grabbed my two bags of camera equipment, Gina and most of the others had hurried across the short stretch of concrete and climbed into the plane. Only the old woman with her pet cage was left outside, heading across the concrete runway. She was a big woman, sturdy, with wide hips that barely fit between the handrails of the boarding ladder. Click: The plane seemed to bow to her as she stepped inside.

I ran the best I could, weighted down with equipment and trying to take a few shots. Click: Empty terminal. Click: Pilot as pale as death, or a haole.

The darkness in the plane made me blink. At the back, the old woman had wedged herself in next to the window, the cage on her lap. "Here," she said, patting the seat next to her, the only empty seat in the plane. For a moment I thought about asking her to switch, but the inside of the plane was so narrow such a move would have required a torturous dance. I took the aisle seat, figuring to shoot across her. Hell, I'd shot over bigger obstacles.

"We have the best seats," the woman said.

"Really?" I buckled in as the pilot angled his way to the cockpit, through students and construction workers packed in, shoulder to shoulder.

"It's smoother here," the woman said. "Lean back. See? You can rest your head against the plane. The others have to sit straight. All the old-timers sit here."

I fiddled with the focus ring on the 28mm.

"I'm taking Blackie, my kitty, home." The woman poked her finger through an air hole in the cage. "It's a horrible problem on the peninsula."

Only half listening, I felt the plane jerk to life, then pivot right as it taxied toward the runway. I closed my eyes. Transitions always scare me.

"Isn't it exciting?" the woman said, patting my knee.

The plane stopped, gathered its strength, and then rushed for the end of the runway.

"Look, you can see the lighthouse," the woman said.

To take my mind off the image of the plane ricocheting off the lighthouse, I asked her, "What problem?"

"Problem?"

"You said there was a problem."

"Too many cats," she sighed, leaning back and resting her head against the vibrating steel.

My stomach dropped as the plane lifted into the air. Christ, cats, yeah, that was a horrible problem, a story that everyone wanted to read.

"Is that your wife?" the woman asked, pointing at Gina.

"My boss."

"Oh, how nice."

The lighthouse grew smaller and smaller.

"And the young ones?" she said, nudging me with her elbow.

"Students from the university. Something to do with historic preservation. They identify boundaries and points of intersection between the natural and the constructed." I wondered which one of them had scribbled Locals Only! on the bathroom door. "You know, rock walls, worn paths, shrub lines, sand dunes. Boundaries. It's a science." I figured that would keep her quiet.

"They should be spayed," she said.

"Who?"

"The cats. The patients don't seem to understand. They find it hard to take that possibility away from anybody."

"What possibility?"

"Having children."

As we flew over the harbor, I remembered the sign posted at the concrete dock. Click: "Warning! No kids. Absolutely, no children under 16 allowed on the peninsula. By order of the law." Kids tend to stare.

"Excuse me," I said, leaning toward the window, twisting the focus ring on the 28mm lens, surprised at how much the buildings, some of them perfectly restored, others poised to collapse, reminded me of Angel Island.

We had gone, Gina and me, to a workshop in San Francisco, something about photojournalism in the age of empire or lawlessness of chaos. Something like that. Angel Island was supposed to be our break, a boat ride, a picnic, a bottle of wine and all that crap and maybe later a chance for something more in the cool Golden Gate air. Instead, Gina had decided to walk to the side of the island where most visitors never went. She had read about the island being used as a detention center for Asian immigrants and she wanted to see what was left. We found a two-story barracks hidden behind eucalyptus trees and a sagging chain-link fence, the same kind of standard issue wood building that populated old army bases and Kalaupapa. Of course, I followed her when she ignored the sign forbidding trespassers. We had to squeeze through a rip in the fence, but the door to the barracks was unlocked. The floors were rotten. A sharp wind off the bay whistled through an endless series of broken windows. Everywhere I looked I saw opportunities for clichéd shots. Click: rotting wood. Click: broken glass. Click: chipped and peeling paint. But nothing new, nothing that I could sell to catch the eye of Americans drowning in an endless stream of images. Gina disappeared into the next room, moving quickly, while I felt my way along the wall of what looked like a communal bathroom, trying to keep from falling through the rotting floor. My hand brushed over a slight indentation. Paint had been peeled off the walls in long strips, revealing another layer of paint that almost covered a message carved into the wall. I licked my finger and used it to rub the dirt out of the crevices. I found three words: I die here. When I looked up I saw more of them. The wall had been used like a huge piece of paper. As I was twisting off the 28mm, I felt someone brush against my shoulder and, startled, I dropped the lens.

"It's the same with the deer," the woman next to me on the plane said.

The plane had reached the top of the cliff. I flicked on the camera's motor drive. "The deer, yeah." The old priest had walked me and Gina into the middle of the deer herd that had forced the inhabitants of Kalaupapa to build fences around their houses. The deer has become so plentiful and fearless they had taken to raiding patients' ornamental plants and small vegetable gardens. One patient had wanted to shoot a few deer as a warning but the others had refused what they called cruelty. So, the three of us had stood in the moonlight, surrounded by deer so unafraid of humans that when we wanted to move, we had to push them out of our way.

There had been deer on Angel Island, too, their huge eyes startled and begging, caught in the flash of my camera and the slow death of starvation. As the plane banked left, heading for Molokai Airport, I set the shutter speed at 1000 to freeze the action.

84

***

The woman looked at his tired face. She was surprised to be sitting next to him. Her friend who sold beer from her carport had told her all about the big haole man with a camera. Three times he had asked her to pose for a photograph as she handed beer to construction workers, and three times she had refused. Even now, she could hear her friend laughing as she described the way he gulped his beers, three of them in less than thirty minutes, so he could finish before the woman he called his boss had finished her swim in the harbor and he could hide behind the old store and aim his camera at her as she dried her body with a thick white towel.

Now, being so close to this man with a secret passion made the woman hunger for the past. She tried to remember herself as a young woman, athletic and strong, dressed in a white cotton shift, the red dust of the peninsula settling on her freshly shampooed hair. She saw her father, a minister from Montana, stepping from the plane on his yearly visit. She had helped him raise money for the settlement and, as promised, he had brought her along to celebrate her eighteenth birthday, to see the miracle of Christ. In the plane now, when she closed her eyes, she could almost see her husband. She rubbed her hands together to feel his skin. A patient without outward signs of the disease, he had met her and her father at the airport and driven them in an old bus to the other side of the peninsula, to show them the work being done on Father Damien's Church. As she stood gazing at the small islets off the jagged coast, the cold wind numbing her nose, she heard him asking her to walk with him that evening. The sun touched her wrinkled fingers, and she could feel his hand, feel the moonlight on her cheek. Nothing ever died. Wasn't that true? She inhaled the sharp smell of the photographer's sweat.

She remembered the town meetings, the baseball leagues, the milk from their dairy. She remembered the state's attempt to close the hospital and move everyone to Oahu. She remembered her husband writing letters to Honolulu to keep the settlement open. She remembered his bandaged hand tapping the typewriter keys. She remembered a time when people, not the Department of Health, the National Park Service, the universities, the federal this and thats made decisions.

Her thoughts went dead for a moment as the plane approached Molokai Airport. Lost in her memories, she thought she could see the rusting fire engine at Kalaupapa that had once seemed so bright and new but had failed them the night the hospital burned down. She wanted to say to this photographer who worked for a newspaper that for thirty years she and her husband had lived in the same house. Now a cook for the construction workers lives in their home. She had been asked to leave after her husband died because was not a patient. She wanted to tell this outsider that she and her husband loved each other, that she should have been allowed to stay in her home where she could feel her husband next to her. She wanted to say, it's not Kalaupapa anymore. But what good were words?

Instead, she imagined herself as a young woman, the daughter of a missionary in paradise, the Tradewinds blowing through the palms, her husband, confessing his fears, then pulling her close to touch his lips to hers. The plane dropped toward the ground, and she saw herself as a young woman, looking up from the ground, pointing at the plane. Her heart stopped. The man was leaning across to shoot a picture out the window.

Click: In a moment, it would all be over.

10. cockfight serenade

three men sat with their backs to the cinderblock wall, unaware they formed a collage of yellow, white, and brown skin. In the shade of a huge orange tree, they shooed away flies as the long afternoon turned to evening.

"Hot today," said Palani, the tallest of the three, and the youngest, though he had reached his fiftieth birthday. He was sitting between his friends, Howard Chang and Bobby Amaral, with his back straight, inhaling the cool scent of orange blossoms.

"Hot, hot, hot," said Chang, squinting into the bright sun.

"Not now," said Bobby. The sun would soon disappear behind the clouds on the mountain.

"Not now," said Palani.

"Not now," said Chang. "Plenty heat earlier." He was a thin man, with short legs and a long trunk. His skin hung from his bones in a way that made the neighborhood kids think of freshly plucked chicken. He lifted his boney hand to block out a ray of light cutting through the tree's branches. "I can still see as good as I did back in the day."

"What can you see?" asked Bobby, kicking a fly off his bare feet.

"Where?"

"Anywhere."

"I see a chicken coop."

"What else do you see?"

"I cannot see anything else."

"Then your eyes are no good," said Bobby, his big hands chasing a fly into the heat. "Lucky you stay retired."

Bobby was a big man, almost as big as Palani, with a round face and a flat nose. He had grown up on a ranch near the top of the volcano and was proud of his country memories, but he had worked most of his life in the pineapple cannery, listening to the clanking and grinding noise of the machinery. For twenty-five years, tiny drops of pineapple juice had fallen from a pipe that refused to be fixed onto the back of his neck, as he stood watching the cans of juice stumbling along the conveyor belt. The juice had stained his shirts and his skin with a sweet scent that ebbed and flowed with the time of day, light and airy in the cool morning, thick and heavy in the warm afternoon, sometimes a hint, now a syrupy suggestion of pineapple, silver cans, and blue labels.

Chang looked under the tree again. "I see," he said, lazily stretching his long thin arms toward the sky, "I see three chicken coops."

Bobby slapped his knee. "Better."

"I see a waste of money."

"Money," said Bobby.

"Money is important.

"Not to me. Me, I see cockfights. What do you see, Palani?"

Palani looked at the chicken coop and thought of the dark insides where the fighting cocks of Mr. Santiago were hiding from the three men. How quiet and cool it must be inside now that the sun is setting.

"Tell us what you see," Bobby said. "Don't be afraid."

"I am not afraid," said Palani. He was a big man with thick shoulders and strong arms from cutting cane, and even strong legs from working in the taro fields. What did he have to fear? Not Bobby. Not Chang. He tried to think again of the fighting cocks but thought instead of the sky. "I see tree branches, and above them I see the sky. The sky is blue and red, and the sun is going down behind the mountains. It will be warm tomorrow. A good day for fishing."

Bobby shook his head. "That is how Hawaiians think. I ask about the chicken coop and he tells me about the sky and fishing."

"I do not want to talk about the chicken coop."

"Why?"

"Nevah mind." He did not want to tell these men that his mind did not always do what he wanted it to do. How could he tell them that his mind had a mind of its own?

"You sound like a child," Bobby said.

"I am not a child."

"I would like to go fishing," said Chang.

Bobby threw his hands in the air. "I give up."

The men pressed their backs against the cinderblock fence, which separated them from a neighborhood built on what had been rolling hills of sand but was now a flat sprawl of affordable ranch-style houses. Herbert Kalanikau and his loud wife lived on one side, the divorced Sandy Cravalho and her two kids on the other, and next to her Mat Madangdang, and across the street Kimo and Jill Matsunaga and their five kids. On every side of every house were more houses. And beyond the houses was the highway, then the cane fields, and beyond the cane fields, at the edge of the ocean, the airport.

The men were resting in the backyard of a cinderblock house with four extra rooms attached. They lived in these rooms and paid rent to an old Filipino man, Mister Alfredo Santiago. They heard a dog bark, a car brake, and smelled the sour hint of car and jet exhaust settling through the branches of the orange tree. They heard a TV blast to life, and old man Kalanikau yell at his son to turn it off. The channel changed, changed, changed again. "Turn it off, boy!" Kalanikau yelled. The channel changed again. A baby cried, and Paiani sighed. To him, all the noise sounded like a kind of music backed up by a cool breeze ruffling the branches of the orange tree and the bamboo Mr. Santiago had planted along the cinderblock fence.

"Sounds like a mountain stream," Palani said, closing his eyes and listening to the wind. "In Waihee Valley."

"What mountain stream?" Bobby said. "I don't hear a stream."

"In the tree."

Chang turned his ear to the sky. "What you hear?"

"I don't hear anything," said Bobby.

"A mountain stream," said Palani.

"A tree is a tree. And the wind is the wind," said Bobby.

Palani wasn't listening. He was watching the sheets hanging on Mr. Santiago's sagging clothesline. The splashed white squares of light, between the green grass and the blue sky. They could be clouds. "Sometimes, the wind in the cane sounds like the ocean. When I was a small boy..."

Bobby inhaled deeply and puffed out his chest. "When you are young, you know nothing, and everything you see is wasted on you because you are too stupid.

Palani tried to make his mind work. He tried to remember his youth, felt the same fear he had felt when he could not think of the fighting cocks.

"Not until you reach forty do you understand life," Bobby said.

"Young people are loud and filled with trouble," Chang said.

As if to prove the point, a young man threw open the back-door of Santiago's house, stepped into the soft light, and slammed the door. "I can't stand it anymore," he shouted across the yard.

For a moment he stood there, tall and skinny, rubbing his eyes and holding a six-pack of beer. Palani organized his thoughts. He knew the man as Michael, a man from the main-land, who worked for the newspaper, doing something. Palani was not sure what. He had a narrow, peach-soft face with blue eyes and lived in the room next to the garage and talked with a strange accent that made the end of his words die very slowly.

"I couldn't sleep," he said. "Too much noise."

"We should be more quiet," Palani said.

"Is that beer?" asked Bobby.

Michael walked across the grass and held out the red and white six-pack. "Not you guys, the TV next door."

Bobby pulled three beers and passed one to each of his friends. "Hmmmm," he said after his first swallow. "I do not listen to noise."

"It is horrible," said Chang, after drinking deeply. "I do not see the point in it."

Palani remembered too late that when he was young his mother had taken him to walk under the eucalyptus trees in Ku-la and the wind in their branches had sounded like an ocean.

"Listen to me," Michael said. "I'm going nuts. Nuts. Nuts!" He paused for a gulp of beer. "Nuts. Nuts. Nuts!"

To Palani the words were as loud as rifle shots.

"I'll go crazy.

I can't sleep.

I can't."

"You get up early, I know that," said Chang, sipping his beer.

"At 3:30. I have to be at work by four."

"That's bad," Bobby said, looking straight ahead. "But a man must do what a man must do."

"That's right," said Chang.

Palani sipped his beer.

"And I can't go to sleep before ten or eleven at night."

"Why is that?" Palani asked.

"Because I can't."

"You should go to sleep earlier," said Bobby.

"I can't."

"You can," said Bobby. "A man has to sleep."

"So I come home at noon for a nap and what happens? What happens?"

The three men waited. All of them liked a good story.

"Santiago stakes his roosters next to my window and they start crowing."

The three men sipped their beers.

"You know, the people at work are crazy. I told them about the roosters and you know what they said? They said isn't it horrible how they wake you up in the morning. In the morning, I said. In the morning! These roosters crow all the time, morning, noon and night."

"Fighting chickens crow all the time," said Bobby.

"Everyone knows that."

"They're not so bad," said Palani.

"What do you know about fighting cocks?" Bobby said. "Hawaiians don't know anything about fighting cocks."

"I know."

"What do you know? Your father was a fisherman," Bobby said.

Michael paced in front of the three old men, waving his beer, drinking, pointing the can at the chicken coop. "They're in there now," he said. "Right in there, in that chicken coop, waiting to torment me. I'll lie down, I'll close my eyes, I'll start to fall asleep, I'll hear the gentle hum of the fan. Then they'll start. Cockadoodledoo. Cock A DOODDLE DOO!" The white man yelled, throwing his arms in the air and crowing at the sky.

Palani tried to imagine this man working at a newspaper. Nothing came to his mind.

"I timed them," Michael said. "He had five of them staked out back here and I heard them screech once every thirteen seconds. Can you believe that? Can you? Once every thirteen seconds?"

Palani did not find it hard to believe that a fighting cock could crow once every thirteen seconds, but he did not say so, because he did not think it worth saying. Fighting cocks crowed all the time, everyone knew that.

"Cocks crow all the time," Bobby said. "Everyone knows that."

"Santiago has no manners. He's inconsiderate. Right next to my window he stakes them. I don't know about you guys, but I pay rent. I could leave, then where would he be? What would he do? No one else is going to pay the rent I pay to live next to a training camp for fighting cocks."

Chang shrugged his shoulders.

"He's Filipino," Bobby said. The big man pulled up one leg, stretched out the other.

"What's that got to do with it?"

"Everything," said Bobby.

"He's right," said Chang.

"Filipinos own fighting cocks," Bobby said, then smiled. "It's their culture."

Palani pored a steady stream of beer down his throat.

"Is that true, Palani?" Michael asked.

"How would he know?" Bobby said, shaking his head. "He's Hawaiian. Isn't that right, Palani?"

Palani nodded.

"And you're Filipino?"

"Do I look Filipino?" Bobby asked.

"No."

"Am I short?"

"No."

"Am I brown? Do I own a fighting cock?"

"Portuguese know everything," Chang said.

The three old men laughed.

"Don't listen to him," Bobby said. "I grew up in the country, I know about fighting chickens."

"I know I hate those roosters," Michael said. "Yesterday, I waited until Santiago went for a walk. I watched from my window and when one of those roosters stuck its head out, I ran out and grabbed the hose and sprayed the hell out of him."

The three men laughed. Palani still could not imagine this man working at the newspaper.

"As soon as I went back in the house, they crowed louder. I told Santiago, I told him, Mr. Santiago, could you please keep those damn chickens quiet? Could you? You know what he said?"

The three men stared at Michael.

"Yes, yes, yes," he said, and then he stakes them out right next to my window, on short lines so they have enough rope to almost reach each other; and they stand there, legs tied to the stakes, stretching their necks at each other, spitting, hissing, flapping their wings, hopping like cripples, crowing and crowing and crowing."

"Good exercise for them that way," Chang said.

"He doesn't work his cocks right."

"Have to walk them, with a stick."

"He doesn't fight those cocks."

"He's too old to fight roosters."

"Those roosters are no good anyways," Bobby said.

Michael leaned toward him. "I untied one and it went after this rooster that was still staked out. They pecked at each other and the guy that was staked out didn't have a chance. He couldn't get off the ground. The free guy jumped on his back and started pecking him, jabbing him in the neck."

"They say old man Santiago has diabetes," Palani said.

"He worked 30 years on the plantation. I know that," said Chang.

The men nodded and drank.

"He worked the irrigation ditches along Puunene."

"Drove that old jeep of his and had his pack of dogs that followed him."

"I remember those dogs," Bobby said, shaking his head and throwing his legs out in a wide V, so that one foot rested in the shade, the other in the dying sun. "They used to follow him along the road, the jeep so slow, and the dogs barking all the time. And they used to sleep in the driveway. Big dogs. Chasing kids. Neighbors always said those dogs get in rubbish and Mr. Santiago should tie them up. He no listen."

Chang nodded.

Palani said, "Always hungry, those dogs. Santiago didn't feed them. They chase kids, too. I seen them. Filipinos don't feed dogs, they eat them."

"Santiago fed his dogs," Palani said.

"Who says?"

"Mister Santiago good with dogs."

"No dogs no more," Chang said.

"I think maybe I'll buy a rooster," Michael said, wondering how the conversation had shifted to dogs. "The biggest meanest rooster I can find, and fight him against Santiago's chickens. I'll kill them all."

Palani stroked the side of his head with a tired hand, as if the motion would wipe away the heavy feeling of the fading afternoon. "Santiago doesn't fight his chickens."

"Too old to fight," said Bobby. "You know that."

"The chickens?" Chang said.

"Him too," said Bobby. "Santiago too old to train fighting cocks."

"Old man needs something to do," said Palani.

"Go fishing, that's what he should do," said Bobby.

"Mr. Santiago not a fisherman," Palani said.

"Everybody is a fisherman," Bobby said.

The three men watched Michael pace from shade to sunshine, sunshine to shade. "I'm going to kill them," he said. "Maybe I'll poison them! I'll put rat poison in their food and Santiago will never figure what happened."

"Don't poison them," Bobby said. "Can't eat them if you poison them. Fighting chicken makes good stew."

"Tough stew," said Chang.

"Not if you cook it right," said Palani. "I know how to cook it right."

"How you know?" Bobby asked.

The screen door at the back of the house opened quietly and slammed shut. The four men looked up to see Mister Alfredo Santiago the proud owner of three fine fighting cocks, standing bowlegged on the cement walkway. For a moment he stood there, letting his eyes adjust to the evening light. With his back bent and his arms hanging stiffly at his side, he squinted vainly at the four dark shapes under the orange tree.

"Hello," Michael said, his voice a nasally razor blade. "Hello, Mister Santiago."

The old man nodded his head and raised his hand a few inches. "Who's that? Who is that with you?"

Bobby leaned toward Palani and said, "Don't get him talking."

"I do not want to hear him to talk," said Chang. "No one can talk as much as this old man."

"Too bad he cannot see as much as he talks," said Bobby.

"He is old and the light is bad," Palani said.

"I'm old and I can see," said Chang.

"You are not as old as him," Palani said.

"No one is that old," said Chang.

"Who is with you?" Santiago asked.

"Why don't you answer him?" Palani said.

The old man shuffled onto the grass, swinging his arms to help his stiff legs move. Slowly, looking at the four men, he stepped into the shade.

"It's me," Palani said.

"I see you," said the old man.

Palani knew that Santiago was lying. The old man's eyes had failed him during the last spring, and now he found his way by memory. Palani could not stop his mind from thinking strange thoughts. How long does it take a man to die? How long before he was as old as Santiago. And who would take care of him? He was a boy and now he was a man. Was the boy dead? Was the boy who crawled into the attic at his mother's house dead? He could not stop himself from remembering. He saw himself finding a dusty box on the day of his tenth birthday, when the rain poured pebble sounds on the tin roof. The box had called to him from a high shelf, promising to reveal great secrets if only he would climb and reach into the dizzying heights. He had stepped from chair to table top, and stood, triumphantly, so high above the ground and near the tin roof that the rain had seemed alive, its pounding the pounding of his heart. But when he reached up, he had grabbed the edge of the shelf and spilled the box into the damp air, causing pieces of paper to flutter down like paper birds in the wind.

His small brown fingers had sifted through the treasure, turning over stiff pieces of paper to find photographs of dark men dressed in baggy black pants and brightly colored shirts. They wore no shoes and were not smiling, as if the photograph had been taken at a moment of great importance. Dogs and chickens stood between their legs. The men stood with their arms crossed in front of sagging, green wooden houses, with thick jungle behind them. On the porch behind them, the women looked very small, with babies held in their arms.

"Feeding the roosters?" Michael asked.

"Yes, yes," Santiago said, as he bent to the ground and pulled a handful of seed from a dirty glass jar. "I always feed."

Palani smelled the pomade the old man used to slick down his patches of hair, and his mind went to work again. He thought of himself as a small boy, and worried that a smell could set his mind wandering. The boy pulled a line that tugged and jerked, until a silver fish poked its head into the air. Then the fish slipped the hook, and disappeared silver into the sharp blue sea. An old man's hand held a blood-stained gaff, exhaust thick at the stern of the small boat. No pomade on the ocean.

Palani heard Santiago's shallow breathing and saw his hands at work, saw wrinkled brown fingers pour a pile of seed in each of the three cups.

"Don't feed those chickens," Michael said, loud enough so that only the three men could hear. "That'll give them more energy. They'll crow more."

Stooped next to the chicken coops, Santiago lifted a nail from the middle latch and opened a small door, letting the nail drop so that it dangled from a dirty string, like a pendulum on a grandfather clock. "My, my, my beauty," he said. "Oh, my big beauty." He reached into the darkness and pulled out a big, almost too big to hold, orange and black cock. He lifted the cock into the air so that a ray of sun found its way to the orange feathers around the cock's neck. "Look how beautiful," Santiago smiled. "See how his feathers are black as night."

Palani remembered a boy's hand touching hot black feathers, feeling rippling heat, as if on fire, and saw a dark eye turning darker.

"You ought to get rid of those cocks," said Bobby. "No good for fighting."

"Plenty good," said the old man.

"What for?"

"For fighting."

"When do you fight them?"

The old man forced the rooster back into the coop.

"You don't fight them," Bobby said.

"They are good fighters."

"How do you know? You don't fight them."

Santiago opened another door and gently lifted into the fading light a smaller rooster with a red crown. "This is a good fighter."

"How do you know?"

"I can see it."

"You cannot see," said Bobby. "He is not a fighter.

"The small kine are the best fighters. I know."

99

"You are right for once," said Bobby. "But none of your cocks are good fighters."

"Do not start him talking," said Chang.

"In the day, my chickens were the best. People from all over knew my chickens. They were good enough to get me a wife."

"You bought a wife with one of your chickens?"

"Not exactly."

"He only wants to talk," said Chang.

"It was not a Maui chicken. It was a Manila chicken."

"See, I told you. He is only talking."

"I have heard of women sold for chickens," said Bobby, nodding. "In the Philippines."

"Yes," Mr. Santiago said. "After the war, and there were no women here, so I flew to the Philippines to my old village."

"You have started him."

"I want to hear the story again," Palani said.

"A man in my village had a daughter."

"That's no surprise," Michael laughed.

"Get to the part about the chicken," Bobby said.

"It was not buying," Palani said.

"It was buying," said Bobby.

"What was buying?"

"This man in my village knew much about arranging things. I believe he had many daughters before this, and he knew me, so he was helpful. He knew about Hawaii and thought me rich, but I was from his village, so he was good to me. He offered me beer to drink, had me sit on his porch. Through the window I saw his daughter sitting at a table, sewing, and I see that she is pretty but not very pretty. That is the way a woman should look. So I ask the man about her, and he says she is a very good daughter, a hard worker, who takes very good care of her father. So I leave, and come back the next day with a pig, for a luau, and the man roasts the pig and the whole village is called to eat with him. The big was fat and juicy, and we all drank beer in its honor."

"What about the chicken?"

"I told you not to get him started."

"After this great feast, does this man offer to arrange something for me and his daughter? No. He lets me sit on the porch and look through the window again. Buttah, I understand because this is the man's last daughter and without her he will be alone; buttah, I am alone and I need a wife and I do not want to feed the old man's village another pig, so I leave and come back the next day with enough beer for the whole village and a new radio for the old man. That night we sit by the fire and everyone drinks beer and we listen to music from Manila and the old man tells me that the village is known for its fighting cocks, and that he owns three of the best fighting cocks in all of the country. We are very drunk, and the next morning, the old man lets me sit on the porch and look through the window again. I am angry and sick, and I would like to shoot this man who refuses to give me his daughter even though I have spent almost all my money on beer and pigs and a PX radio. I do not want to go home without a wife, one who is from the country and will like living on Maui and not want to move to the big city, like Honolulu. Many girls from the Philippines want to live in the city. So I leave and take the next bus to Manila, and I spend three days searching the markets for the perfect gift to show my respect. When I get back, I place a new traveling cage on the man's porch and point at the bird inside."

Santiago hit his chest with his fist so hard that Palani thought he would fall down.

"I tell the old man that this fighting cock is the last gift I will bring and that I have no more money to give him, and that if the old man wants his daughter to be a wife of a good man, with a house in the States, he'd better do it now, because if not, I, Alfredo Santiago, will go back to the United States and be forced to find a white wife, or a Japanese wife, or a Hawaiian wife. She will not be as beautiful as his daughter but a man cannot be alone."

Bobby said, "You talk a good deal."

"He talks a lot," Chang said.

"Sometimes it is good to talk big when what you have is small. There were no women on Maui for a Filipino man. Buttah, I was hoping he knew chickens, and I had purchased the perfect fighting chicken. Any man who knew fighting chickens could see that. This Manila chicken was small but strong with big lungs and a huge heart. I left the fighter on the porch and I walked off."

Santiago waited until the young man from the newspaper leaned forward, then he said, "The old man ran after me and thanked me for the fighting cock, the most beautiful fighting cock he had ever seen. He said he would be dead soon, but until then he loved his daughter so much he didn't want to lose her, so he begged me to wait until his death, a matter of months, a year at the most, he was an old man, he said. Only then I could have his daughter. What else was there for me to do? I agreed, and two years later the old man died, and the daughter came here to be my wife."

"Mrs. Santiago?" said Michael.

"She is a good woman," said Santiago. "No one can say otherwise."

"A strong woman," said Palani.

"She does not talk too much," said Chang. "I can see why she treats your chickens so kindly."

"And she is young enough to take care of you," said Bobby.

"She takes good care of me," said Santiago. He gently placed the small cock in its coop. "She loved her father and she loves me. She will take care of me."

"How can you buy a woman?" asked Michael.

"Many people do it," said Bobby. "It is not so bad. Sometimes it goes wrong. That can happen. I have seen it happen."

"It's not love," said Michael. "He didn't know her. He didn't ask her."

"It is not buying," said Palani.

The big cock popped its head into the light and pecked at the yellow seeds, stopped, stretched its necks to watch the old man. Pecked, stopped. Looked right. Looked left, pecked, watched the old man walk across the grass, pecked. Watched knee-high rubber boots flapping against old boney legs. Watched shorts and faded red t-shirt flapping on the old man's thin body. Pecked. Pecked. Pecked at the yellow seed.

"All wives and husbands are bought," said Bobby.

"She will take care of me," said Santiago as he opened the screen door. When it banged shut, the rooster jerked its head into darkness.

"He bought Mrs. Santiago with a rooster?"

"She is a good woman," said Palani. "It is something you cannot understand."

"You can?" Bobby laughed.

"I hate those roosters," Michael said.

He walked to the side of house, picked up a broom, and marched deep into the darkness under the orange tree.

"I'm going to kill one. He'll never miss one."

"He'll miss it," Palani said. "Or she will."

The big rooster stuck its head out, saw Michael, and ducked back into darkness. "There's no place in this world for roosters," said Michael. He pointed the blunt end of the broomstick at the dark hole.

"Plenty of place for roosters if you're an old Filipino man," Palani said.

"Look at this Hawaiian defending a Filipino man," said Bobby.

"Let's kill one," Michael said.

"My father killed plenty," Chang said.

"You ever been to one cockfight?" Bobby asked.

"Not that I remember," Michael said.

"You'd remember a cockfight," Bobby said.

"They're barbaric."

"What's that?"

"For uncivilized people," said Michael.

"Who's that?"

"Uncivilized people are people who fight cocks. Everyone knows that."

"Everyone?" said Chang.

A cool breeze ruffled the feathers of the orange tree. Palani looked at the ground. He remembered a plantation house and a dusty road with cane fields on both sides, a sea of cane waving in the breeze. An irrigation ditch flowed behind the house and a boy of twelve sat with his feet dangling in the dark water that seemed to him a river with hidden secrets. A dog barked, and the boy jumped to his feet and ran along the irrigation ditch, arms pumping, like he had seen the runners at the county fair do. Racing on the dirt track, their eyes searched for the finish line. He climbed a steep embankment to the dirt road and waited there until he saw a small brown Filipino man, walking slowly away from the camp houses. "Uncle, take me with you," the boy said, catching the man and holding onto his hand.

"Ah, buttah," the Filipino man said. "And what will you tell your mother?"

"I no tell."

"You would lie to my sister?"

"Not a lie."

The two of them walked together, kicking up dust.

"If she asks, you must tell the truth."

"I will. But only if she asks."

They found a circle of men behind the last house in the camp. The men were dressed in shirts, long pants and polished shoes. They squawked, waved fists filled with money, moved around the circle, slapping each other on the back, pointing at the two men inside the circle. Each of the two held a fighting cock. One man whispered to his bird, kissed its head, stroked its feathers. The other man held his bird at arm's length and did not speak.

The boy's uncle leaned over and whispered to the boy, "I will bet on the quiet bird."

The boy smelled beer and cigars on his uncle. He too liked the quiet one, because it had shiny black feathers on its head and tail. A man shouted. For a second the circle became quiet. Then the two cocks flew at each other, wings flapping, claws in the air. The boy's uncle waved his arms and shouted for the black-tailed rooster to fight like a man. And the boy saw the enemy of the black-tailed rooster jump high in the air and come down clawing at the black-tailed rooster's neck. The enemy jabbed, jabbed, jabbed its beak. The men yelled and pointed and squeezed the circle tight around the two fighters, and the air smelled of dust and something wet, something that reminded the boy of his finger cut on barbed-wire.

Michael could not stand the silence. "I wouldn't mind eating these roosters, all of them," he said.

"You have to cook them a long time," said Chang.

"I don't care."

"When I was a small boy," Palani said, "my uncle would take me to watch the cockfights. After, he would bring a chicken to my mother and she would boil it for a long time to make stew. We sat in the kitchen and I picked the meat from the stew with my fingers, and my uncle drank cold beer with beads of sweat on the glass. That was after my father, Peter Kalanikau, was killed on the reef at Waihee. My mother was a Filipino woman. She had worked the plantation cutting cane. When she was ill, and my father was gone, my uncle took care of us. He came to watch the house in the evenings and make sure we had enough to eat. He was a good Filipino man."

The four men in the backyard of Mr. Santiago's house were quiet for a moment. Then Chang looked at the monkey orange tree, and said, "I hear wind in the tree."

"It is a stream in the mountains," Palani said.

"It is the ocean," said Bobby.

"I see it," said Chang.

"What?" asked Michael.

11. journal entries

December 3
Number 1

After reading Joey's journal, I'm hiding in the darkroom, behind two locked doors. For extra protection, I have switched on the red warning light. Stay Out! It blinks in the hall of the Communication Building. Developing in Progress!

I am safe from hundreds of college students whispering, circling, and plotting. I am safe. That may not sound like a very good attitude for a teacher, but I'm not exactly a teacher. I'm a photograph, an 8x10 black-and-white photograph.

December 3
Number 2

What a comfortable sensation being flat. Seconds ago, or was it hours? my body had depth. I could move. I could rest my head against the Durst enlarger, stretch my legs to the plastic developing trays, even wiggle my toes. With each new breath, my lungs expanded. They were beach balls, stretched, about to deflate.

Now, though, I am flat. Is it a crime? No, of course not. After all, I am not pornography. I am a black-and-white portrait of a middle-aged man going bald, wearing a faded aloha shirt, dark slacks and rubber slippers.

Being flat has all the advantages of being three-dimensional, but none of the nasty side effects. I can hear the ticking of the Nikon timer. I see my coffee, bitter and black. I can even feel the heat rising from the styrofoam cup. The steam brushes along my archival skin, rises to my lips, touches my nose. (The smell reminds me of ferricyanide, the acid I use to lighten prints.) All this, and I do not have to fear discovery. Here, inside this picture, I am safe.

There is, though, one problem. I can see Joey's journal open on my lap.

December 3
Number 3

I am a picture of tired hands, ring finger missing, holding Joey's journal open to page 33: MR. VINCENT, I WANT A PICTURE OF ME AND THE MAN I LOVE. I WANT PEOPLE TO UNDERSTAND.

December 3
Number 4

This is my fault. Not Joey's sex life. That is not my fault, but my knowledge of it. The other teachers, the old-timers, warned me not to read the journals. Too much work, they said. Not enough time, they said. Simply a departmental formality for Writing Intensive courses, they said. Count the entries, make sure there are fifty, forget reading them. They said that the students cheated, anyway, and wrote all the entries on the last day.

Why didn't I listen? Because I was a fool. Because I was a rookie, a substitute for a regular lecturer who had fallen ill, and because I imagined myself, severed finger and all, a newspaper photographer with a fully developed thick skin. Besides, is there any doubt about photographers? We are voyeurs, the lot of us. I admit it.

So I read every page, peeked through every window, saw Joey eating greasy fries, saw him leaning back in the front row of a Christian Slater movie, saw the buses passing, the coffee beans in Safeway, the wet sidewalks in Wailuku. Saw his hands touch

December 3
Number 5

No more of that. Staring, after all, is what got me into trouble in the first place. Besides, any scene of explicit sex is strictly in my imagination. In truth, Joey's journal, except for his lines on page 33, is quite mundane, ordinary, although slightly sentimental.

Only page 33 hints of real emotion.

On page 33, stains have smeared his words.

At first, I thought that the page had been stained by tears. The page had wrinkled in spots, as a letter to a loved one might. I imagined myself having to stare at these tear stains for the rest of my life, which, considering the shelf life of archival paper, could have been a hundred, two hundred years. An eternity. In the darkroom, for the rest of time, I would sit below my award-winning photograph of Billie Paka, and I would dream of love. This would be, I believed, a fittingly dramatic and ironic end to my life.

Then my nose, flat but still conscious of its physiological purpose, had inhaled a distinctly eastern odor. What could it be? I shook myself free, raised the journal to my nose. The stains on the page were not tears. They were soy sauce! No doubt Joey had hunkered over his journal in a Chinese restaurant, stuffing heaps of beef broccoli into his mouth as he plotted my involvement.

Now, Billie is hanging next to me on the wall. His face, thanks to the firm grip of black-and-white photography, has not lost its youthful charm. He is sharp angles, shadows and light. He is a violent promise.

I took that picture of him when I was twenty-five, and I have kept it all these years. Believe me, it has paid the rent. Notice the dime-size splatters below his eye, across his cheek? Black-and-white photography makes my blood appear so much more real, don't you think? Now the two of us will hang together in our archival years. I wonder what he feels, this man who mixed his passions with so much pain, about a young man, still a boy, who mixes his words of love with soy sauce?

What, he might say to me, has become of love?

December 3
Number 6

I never thought of Joey as the type to confess. He seemed too ordinary, too introverted, too large.

In class, he sits near a window at the back, quiet, not handsome, not ugly, almost bright, almost bored, perfectly camouflaged. He has only one distinguishing characteristic, his size and a glaring weakness for wearing, habitually, a particularly outlandish Hawaiian shirt. Every Friday he appears like a sunrise, adorned in cheap rayon, a huge flash of red and orange pineapples and pink Eskimos grasping slightly sagging fishing poles.

What does it mean?

Before reading his journal, I imagined his shirt a passing fancy, a Freudian slip, a joke. He would outgrow it, buy instead a Bank of Hawaii uniform, sit behind a desk in penny loafers, slacks and a conservative blue aloha shirt. The Eskimos would be safely hidden in a secret drawer at home, beneath his favorite pair of underwear. Now, I am not so sure.

December 3
Number 7

How can I help him? What do I know about love? Forty-five years ago, my father pressed the shutter release, produced my negative. Slowly, arduously, my mother twisted the ancient knobs of her enlarger, exposing me to light until I appeared on a page of Kodak resisto high gloss paper. The doctors washed me in a river of Versatol. In hypo-neutralizer, on a thousand Sunday afternoons, I hardened. I swam in acid-stop-bath streets crowded with three-dimensional characters, deadlines, headlines, and denials. Men, except for one, took no interest in me, and women (there were a few), fled after seeing that I was paper-thin. Until, at last, I surfaced in this peaceful pool, this fresh rinse of college life.

Now I am no longer out of place. I am a finished product. I am safe. But somewhere out there, Joey is still alive, developing. He is hunting me. I will tell him when he comes that I have no knowledge of the three-dimensional movements required for love. I am a photograph.

December 3
Number 8

Billie Paka, now there was a man who knew about love. I remember, in particular, his lips. Thick and full, they reeked of glamorous cruelty the night we first met. I remember that I focused my Nikon FM2 on the wet crease of his nicotine-stained teeth. Did I think it was funny, he asked, that we were meeting in a church across the street from the police station?

Tall and thin, naked to the waist, he could have been a model in an advertisement for tight jeans or unisex cologne. So many people wanted him, to photograph him, to interview him, to split open his head. Was I to be the lucky one?

He said he liked my work but he was disappointed that my front-page photo of Eddie Matland had not captured the look of true sexual joy Eddie had experienced at the moment of death.

It's like this, Billie said, I want you to take a picture of me. I want the world to see the real me, not a mug shot of a fuckin' criminal. You show them, how I felt. How I felt as I stabbed Eddie the fuckin' fag.

I focused the lens on his lips, settled my finger on the shutter release.

Not yet, he said. You have to wait.

Billie had moved closer, until our shoulders were touching. His breath licked my cheek, my ear. Do you feel it? he whispered. I sat still and cool, the professional. It was my job to snap a picture of the murderer before his arrest.

He kissed my cheek, my chin, while I held the camera to my eye. His tongue grazed my ear. His hand moved up my thigh, stopped. Here, he said, and gently took my hand away from the camera. You're trembling. Are you sure you can hold the camera steady?

He pressed his lips to my fingertips, slid my ring finger into his mouth. Then he jerked his head away. Smiling, he said, you like it, don't you, you sick fag. In one quick move, he pinned my wrist to the wooden pew. Fag, he said, and flicked open the knife. The tip of the blade punctured my skin. He pressed the steel through. Jammed it through my knuckle. Slowly. Until at last, unable to move, frozen, stiff, I saw the sudden burst of red.

Now, he said, sitting back, wiping his hand across his cheek, Take my picture.

That Billie, he knew all about love. He was an artist.

December 3
Number 10

My development is not yet complete. The feeling of flatness comes and goes. A moment ago I could write.

Now I can walk on the tile floor. In the developing closet, I find Joey's film, and hold it to the light, let it pass before my eyes, like the windows of a train in the night. I see a young man, a stranger in a baseball cap. No doubt, this is Joey's lover. I see him looking over his shoulder. Now he is standing at the beach, his pants rolled above his ankles. Now he is standing outside a Chinese restaurant.

The negative reminds me of photographs taken on vacation. The young man is stiff in each shot, at center stage. He is poor composition, with no thought to art. And Joey has made another serious mistake. The shots, most of them, are slightly out of focus. He forgot to hold the camera steady while pressing the shutter release. Instead of squeezing the trigger, he jerked it.

There is, though, one shot that might be saved. In the last frame, the young man is balanced on a rock wall, arms stretched out, like wings, and he is looking up, the sun in his face, as if he is about to take flight.

Wait.

Someone is knocking at the door.

December 3
Number 11

Joey's journal lies open on my lap, and I can see my reflection in the brown bottles of developing fluid. A drop of sweat waits to role down my cheek. In the trash, Joey's negatives, swirl and hiss, like snakes. How long have I been sitting here? An hour? Ten minutes? A year? Clocks do not move in photographs. Water drops hang on brass faucets, forever. Another knock.

December 3
Number 12

Joey's fingers crawl, tarantula-like, from behind the door. A slippered foot appears, then a bare knee, plaid shorts, and Eskimos. His face flashes white. "Mr. Johnny?" he says, attempting a smile a moment too late, as if surprised, caught by a strobe, overexposed. "Why didn't you answer the door?"

My lips are squeezed shut, holding back a mouthful of archival paper and Versatol.

He points his Nikon at me, twists the lens, a 105 zoom. "I knocked a hundred times. Finally, the janitor came by. Wait. Sit still." He clicks off three shots. "Got you."

Sit still? Do I have a choice? Why is it so hard for him to see the obvious? The oblivious?

A child on an ice flow, he steps across the tile floor. "I need your help," he says. Eskimos passing shelves of chemicals, jerk their poles, make orange fish dance on silver hooks.

"Mr. Vincent." His fingers slide up a bottle filled with Ferricyanide, and for an instant I feel as if I am a genie, awaiting his command. "I have this picture," he says, "that I want to develop for my class project. A picture of my friend...my best friend."

He scratches his ear, flicks on the safelight, drowns us in red. How cool he is, how much like a future professional. But after he leans forward and flicks the enlarger switch, the soft light rises to the face of a child leaning forward to blow out candles on a birthday cake.

Now he's looking up at Billie Paka. "I want to take a picture like that one, Mr. Vincent." His finger touches Billie's chin. "Did you use tri-X?"

What is it about Billie that so attracts the innocent? His lips? His beauty. His unspoken promise of cruelty?

Joey, on his tiptoes, stretches up, as if to reach his father's face. "There's so much grain," he says, looking into Billie's eyes. "You must have been in the dark."

The two of them are about to kiss. Of course, why didn't I see that before? Joey has planned it all along. "Don't touch," I shout, loud enough to shake the chemicals in the developing trays.

Eyes wide, Joey steps back. (I can see now that he has never believed in the danger of photographs. No doubt he thinks they are simply made of chemicals and paper.)

"We were in a church," I say. "At night, by candlelight. See the reflection of the candles on his cheek? You need a steady hand in that kind of light to get a good picture," I say, digging his negatives out of the trash.

"He looks real."

"He is real."

"It's the black and white," Joey says. "The black-and-white lends an air of realism."

"No, he's real. He's a real fuckin' faggot."

Joey's mouth makes an O, and for a second he is a photograph. He can't move. I hand him his negatives.

"That faggot taught me a lesson," I say. "Even though I wanted to puke when I focused on him, I held my camera steady.

Even when he was smearing my blood on his face, I held my camera steady. And now look at him. Perfectly clear."

He holds the negatives s to the light but he's not looking at them, he's looking through them, at me. "They're out of focus," I say. "All of them. Come back when you're not so excited about your subject." I toss him his journal. "I didn't have time to read it. Bring it back when you have some decent shots."

Joey learns fast. He's backing toward the door. He sees me now as I have always been, an 8X10 black-and-white photograph, lacking color, very thin.

Billie would have been proud of me.

December 3
Number 13

How good it feels to run with my camera in my hand. The air smells clean, like a newly opened package of Kodak paper. For a second, as the bright sunlight hits me, I feel my fingers hardening on my motordrive. Perhaps I should sit on the grass under the banyan tree, return to the still life, harden into a photograph of a middle-aged professor resting in the shade. No, the idea is to keep running, don't stop, don't stand still, run until the day is a memory.

Then I hear tired brakes fighting hard, a horn that will not stop. I run toward a tangle of cars that has blocked the entrance to the college. Pushing through the bystanders, I realize they have the sullen faces of critics at a bad movie. I step off the sidewalk, expecting to see Joey bleeding on the black asphalt.

But he is alive. He is kneeling over a young man. He drops his journal and his camera. He slips his hand under the man's neck, pinches the man's nose.

Through my telephoto lens, I see that the man's hair is thick and sticky, like cotton candy. Behind me, a woman chatters, explaining to a policeman how she saw the two young men standing at the corner, waiting for the light to change, when for no reason, the one with the baseball cap ran.

I focus on the red pickup truck with the smashed front end, the shattered window. I hear my insides ticking. I have gears and springs. I am mechanical. I am a timer waiting to click in the darkroom.

Joey blows air into the man's mouth, coughs, turns his head, and spits blood on the asphalt. The blood is black.

Kneeling on broken glass, I focus on Joey's fingers where they touch the man's lips.

"Please," Joey' says, "help me. Give me something for his head."

I hold the camera steady. Unable to move.

Joey's fingers, spotted with blood, grab the journal, shove it under the boy's cotton candy hair.

Click.

Now Joey's friend lies hardened and still, staring at the sky as if he sees something only he can see, a place to go, a place to hide. But he cannot move. He cannot run, walk, amble, strut.

He is a photograph.

12. a case of mistaken
identity

---

mr. Manlapit's jeep woke to the rusty taste of a dream rattling through its radiator. In the fifty years since it had rolled off the Willys assembly line, the jeep had dreamed only three times. Each time the dream had been the same. Without a driver, the jeep would drop from the clouds and fly gracefully over a sea of tulips as big as army helmets. The next day, after waking to the same rusty taste, the jeep would lose a close friend never to be seen again.

The jeep wanted to kick itself. Dreams were for men, not machines. It was a United states jeep, serial number 345673, equipped with government issue four-cylinder engine and four wheel drive, an exact copy of the prototype test-driven by Dwight D. Eisenhower when the future president was a lieutenant colonel in the U.S. Army. It was built to roar through mud, survive the severest snowstorm, and charge through hurricanes at a top speed of thirty-nine miles per hour. It was not built to dream.

It believed only what it could touch and see, right here, right now, in Mr. Manlapit's driveway. Tires resting on hot asphalt, the jeep felt Mr. Manlapit twist off its radiator cap. His rough and stiff fingers made the jeep remember an army auction in Kahului forty-five years ago. Mr. Manlapit had appeared from the shade of a banyan tree. At first the jeep had not liked the wiry little man. He was much shorter than anybody in the Fifth Reconnaissance Brigade, so short he had to stand on tiptoes to look under the jeep's hood, and his rubber boots and bright red T-shirt were not government issue. The jeep liked khaki uniforms and shaved heads smelling of gun powder, not faded jeans and thick black hair brushed straight back, plastered in place with sweet smelling pomade. Then Mr. Manlapit had caressed its dented fender and brushed the cane dust off its odometer, saying "I'll save you, old friend."

Now, the jeep felt Mr. Manlapit's tiny hands push a stiff hose down its radiator. The jeep sniffed the air, smelled cane smoke and Mr. Manlapit's pomade, and something else, something sweet and sickly. Battery acid dripped onto its starter wire, as cool water rushed through its hoses. The water made the jeep think of the ocean off Charley Young's Beach, where, as a raw recruit, it had charged ashore with Colonel Blackman. The Colonel's hands were army hands, heavy and slow, with knuckles the size of lug nuts. With only one of them gripping his steering wheel, the jeep had led a grand, simulated assault, until a wave had smashed into its rear end and thrown the Colonel into the sea. As the jeep's wiring had hissed and sizzled, the colonel had surfaced, waving his .45 and yelling, "Hit the beach! Make death dance on their graves!"

The jeep heard Mr. Manalpit's rubber boots scraping on the asphalt. "Death is a thief," the old man whispered. A drop of his sweat hit the hot concrete.

Who is death? the jeep wondered. Had it danced with Colonel Blackman and Mrs. Manlapit? Was it looking for Mr. Manlapit's son? The jeep wanted to understand but it was only a jeep.

Jagged fingernails scraped across its canvas top. "Yikes, this sucker is old," a strange voice said. "War surplus, right?"

At first the jeep thought Mr. Manlapit's son had returned from the war in the desert, but when it looked in the rearview mirror, it saw that the man's green eyes swimming in a pool of white skin and freckles. How long had he been hiding back there? The jeep, shaking and shivering, searched the glove compartment for Mr. Manlapit's lucky dog tags, the ones he had worn in the Korean War, but the glove compartment was empty except for a layer of rust.

"Why all the batteries?" the stranger said, brushing his fingers through his red hair. He rubbed cold hand along a dent in the jeep's fender. "Wire problems, right" he peered under the hood with Mr. Manlapit. "My friends call me Stretch."

Mr. Manlapit, short and stocky in his bright red Maui Land And Pine t-shirt, rubbed his hands clean on his cutoff jeans before taking the younger man's hand. He was only a boy, really, not much older than his son.

Stretch pumped Mr. Manlapit's hand. "This is the first time I've ever been to this side of the island. Dream City, right? Kinda funny that name. Ha, ha, ha, ha!" He dropped Mr. Manlapit's hand and pointed past the last row of cinder-block houses, at the cane fire across the street. "Must be pretty hard to breathe round here. Ha ha."

To the jeep, his laughter sounded like machine gun fire. What was wrong with cane smoke? the jeep wondered. Cane smoke meant work, and work was good for men and jeeps.

"Buttaah," Mr. Manlapit said, rubbing the dog tags dangling from his neck.

"Hey, what's the matter? You okay? You look kinda tired." The boy brushed a lock of wild red hair out of his eye.

"Ghosts everywhere," Mr. Manlapit whispered.

"What did you say, old man?"

The jeep did not understand. Were ghosts and death the same thing? Was this strange young man a ghost? And if he was a thief, what did Mr. Manlapit have worth stealing? There was only his old house and his fighting cocks. The house was old and made of cinder blocks in a neighborhood next to the airport, and the fighting cocks were no good for fighting because Mr. Manlapit's son was no longer here to train them. So what could death steal?

"Hey, anybody else home?"

The jeep felt the man slap his fender, and heard him hiss, "Someone who speaks English? You understand? The jeep! I want to buy it." A long finger poked through a rust spot in the jeep's hood. "Beautiful," the young man said. "How about a test drive?"

It was obvious to the jeep that this man with his head on fire did not want to buy anything. A man bargaining for a used jeep did not call it beautiful. Besides, couldn't this boy see that Mr. Manlapit would never sell the jeep? The old man and the jeep were best friends, and Mr. Manlapit had promised to give the jeep to his son when he returned from the war.

"Buttaah," Mr. Manlapit said, shuffling his rubber boots along the hot pavement, pointing at two batteries on the grass, "wires no good."

"I love this dent," the Stretch man said, running his finger over the wound that Corporal Smith, drunk with dreams of victory and a girl named Lina, had smashed into the jeep's front fender on New Year's Eve 1945. The corporal's thick aftershave had smelled of Spam and whiskey the night he replaced the jeep's headlights, saying that it was a mistake to think about death, because when you thought about death, you got dead.

"Cool, this dent."

Cool? Another lie. The jeep had been sitting in the sun all day. It's skin was as hot as cane fire. The Stretch kicked the four bald tires. "Originals?" he asked, his face exploding into laughter, freckles flying in a hundred directions. "Ha, ha," he slapped Mr. Manlapit on the back. "Just kidding."

The jeep felt the boy's cold breath on its radiator cap, his slippery fingers tugging at its ignition wires.

"Hey," Stretch said, popping up like a jack-in-the-box. "This engine is clean. Really clean." He reached inside the cab, and his greasy fingers rubbed against the odometer's dusty glass. "Fifty-six thousand miles? I'm impressed."

Why didn't Mr. Manlapit speak up? Why didn't he tell death about the jeep's war wound? Tell him the jeep had stayed on Maui during two wars because its wiring had been ruined by exposure to salt water? Why didn't Mr. Manlapit say the jeep was unreliable instead of standing in his boots, scratching his head and saying what he always said when he was trying to think? "Buttaah."

"See, I'm driving this rental car," Stretch said, and pointed at a tiny Toyota parked next to the sidewalk. "It makes me look like a tourist. Understand? I'm not a tourist, I'm a reporter. Got the job last week. Flew in from San Francisco. I need a local car, a Maui cruiser. This jeep has character."

The jeep could not believe Mr. Manlapit was smiling, a weak little scratch of a smile, but still a smile, something it had not seen since Mrs. Manlapit disappeared into the hospital. "Yes, yes, yes," Mr. Manlapit said. "My jeep has character."

"Don't worry. I'll take care of it like it was family, like it was my son." Patrick patted him on the back. "Hey, don't look so beat, old guy. I'll give you three hundred bucks."

The jeep felt death's bony butt plop down in the driver's seat. "Stand clear," Stretch yelled, his knees hugging the steering wheel.

The jeep dug its tires into the asphalt, and when death jerked the ignition switch, it squeezed its wires into tight knots. Click, click, click, click. Stretch slapped the steering wheel. "Damn, dead battery."

"Wiring no good," whispered Mr. Manlapit.

"I'll give you two hundred bucks. Ha, ha."

Stretch jumped out of the jeep, kicked the front tire. "Don't worry. I can fix it."

Before the jeep could let the air out of its leaking front tire, death had run down the driveway, lifted the Toyota's hood, and run back with a big black battery the size of an ammo box. "Bingo," he snapped, muscles in his arms and neck bulging. "Bingo, Baby."

The jeep watched Mr. Manlapit wave aftershave out of his face. Tell him the truth, the jeep wanted to scream. Tell him that the neighborhood will not be able to wake up if they do not hear the click, click, click of its dead batteries. Tell him about the hundred Saturday afternoons your son spent hunting for shorts in the wiring. Tell him that a war wound never heals. Death plopped his battery on the jeep's injured fender, and the jeep saw two words stamped in dull red ink between the battery's silver terminals: NEVER DIE. "Guaranteed for life," Stretch laughed, ripping out the old battery and dropping it on the grass, where it landed with a thud. "Bury it."

"Never die," Mr. Manlapit said, touching the new battery with one finger, lightly, as if it contained a hidden secret.

No, the jeep wanted to scream. Stretch squeezed the NEVER DIE into the jeep, and, tightening the cables with Mr. Manlapit's rusty wrench, yelled, as if Mr. Manlapit were deaf, "Now, you'll see how a real battery works."

"Buttah."

Stretch wiped his hands on the jeep's fender, grabbed Mr. Manlapit's elbow and pushed him toward the passenger seat. "Test drive. Come on. One little test drive won't kill you."

The jeep felt Mr. Manlapit shaking as he settled onto the worn springs, and when the old man touched the windshield to steady himself, the jeep remembered Colonel Blackman's hands the day the corporal had driven him to Kahului Harbor to watch the soldiers march up a catwalk, past canvas-covered lifeboats, into a gray ship. The jeep, listening to the wind brushing over the lifeboats, had dozed off, and for the first time, had dreamed of flying over a sea of white tulips as big as army helmets. Now, the jeep felt death's fingers on the ignition switch, and before it could tangle its wires death had yanked the switch.

The current sizzled through its frayed wires. The jeep felt young again. It remembered Manlapit's boy, no taller than a tire, and saw the road to Kihei, waves of heat rising from the asphalt. It remembered the wind blowing through the hole in the canvas top, making the sound of a flag flapping in the wind, and remembered the boy's little butt bouncing on the worn springs. It saw Mr. Manlapit's hand on the boy's knee, saw the beach where it had charged ashore, saw Mr. Manlapit's fishing pole stuck in the sand, saw the boy reach into the bait bucket, pick up a papio, silver and blue, and hold it to his ear, listening for life.

No more stay life stay, Mr. Manlapit had told the boy.

The jeep shook itself free of memories as death pressed on the gas and drove into the street. Cinder-block houses rushed by in a blur. Mr. Manlapit's hand turned white against the windshield. A stop sign appeared. The jeep screeched, locking its brakes and skidding to a stop on the white line, snapping death's head into the windshield.

"Ouch, whiplash!" Stretch said, rubbing his forehead.

"Battery no good. Buttaaah, brakes good."

"Hey, no harm, no foul. See any marks? Any damage? How do I look?"

The jeep thought death looked stupid, too tall, with his carrot-colored hair pressed against the canvas.

Stretch stomped on the gas, jerked the steering wheel hard right, and shot into traffic, squeezing in between an old station wagon and a pink pickup truck.

Honk! Honk! HONK! the pickup yelled.

Where, the jeep wondered, had death learned to drive? Didn't he know that a jeep had a narrow wheelbase and had to be steered gently around turns?

"Ha, ha, ha, ha!" Stretch threw his arms in the air as if he were a kid riding a roller coaster. "Let's see if this jeep has any life left. Let's see if it can pass a fat old station wagon."

The jeep felt its steering wheel twisted hard left, and suddenly it was charging at oncoming traffic, its speedometer shivering, fluttering, climbing past twenty-nine. In the back of the station wagon, a big black German dog snapped its yellow teeth while a hole in the station wagon's muffler coughed. A cane haul truck, as big as a bus and growing bigger, charged toward the jeep. Death's flat foot pressed the gas. The speedometer struggled to thirty-six, thirty-seven, thirty-eight, thirty-nine, but refused to go any further. What did death want to do? Didn't he know the jeep's military specifications? Thirty-nine miles per hour was its top speed. Period. Even with a hundred cars lined up behind him honking their horns, the jeep would never go faster than thirty-nine.

The truck grew to the size of three buses stacked on top of each other, and still the jeep refused to pass the station wagon, even when its driver, a young man with purple hair, flipped a finger at them as a signal to pass. The jeep felt death kick the gas pedal to the floor. But the jeep held steady at thirty-nine. Death had to be taught a lesson.

"Go for it!" Stretch yelled.

"Buttaaaaaah."

The jeep shook and rattled over the bumpy road as the cane haul truck grew to the size of ten, twenty, a hundred buses stacked on top of each other. The jeep smiled at the elephant ear trees, trunks thicker than telephone poles and skin as smooth as marble as they reached their branches over the road. The jeep knew this road, the road Mr. Manlapit had driven for more than thirty years on his way to the sugar cane mill. They were crossing their swords to welcome Mr. Manlapit, shedding shadows as if they were tears dark and cool on his face, and the jeep remembered how gently Mr. Manlapit had always pressed the gas pedal, even on Friday nights when he had driven deep into the cane, the boy's black dog in the back, to the circle of cars parked with lights on and engines running, where the jeep had watched Mr. Manlapit's son step from light into darkness, holding Champion, the biggest of Mr. Manlapit's fighting cocks, blood dripping from the bird's neck and falling onto the boy's shaking fingers.

Death twisted the jeep's steering wheel, strangling it, and the jeep, still going thirty-nine, jumped over the white line as the station wagon swerved off the road and a blinding swoosh of wind and flying rocks rushed by, pulled along by the cane haul truck. "Wow! Great!" Stretch yelled as a stalk of sugar cane six-feet long crashed into the windshield and flew over the canvas top.

"Buttaah, my jeep is good."

In its rear view mirror the jeep saw the station wagon glance off an elephant-ear tree, shake itself like a dog shaking off water, and stagger back onto the road. Honking horns and grinding gears and Patrick's "Ha ha ha!" hung in the air like one of Corporal Bracket's drunken songs. But the jeep was not listening. It was watching Mr. Manlapit. The jeep had never seen his face so alive with strange currents. Not even when he was a young man had his face seemed so full of strength and courage, so alive and mysterious. It reminded the jeep of the boy's face when he had sat with the girl, watching the sunset. Face afire, Mr. Manlapit pointed at the light reflected red off the windows of houses high on the volcano.

"There," he said. "Drive there."

"You think this thing can make it up the mountain, old man?" Stretch laughed and threw his hands in the air. "Sure, the volcano." He slapped the steering wheel. "Why didn't I think of that? This baby needs an uphill test drive."

Radiator boiling, engine rattling, the jeep followed the gently curving road through the cane fields and up the side of the volcano, into the cool air alive with the smell of eucalyptus. No matter how hard death pressed the gas pedal, the jeep navigated each turn with care, no faster than fifteen miles per hour, so slow that a parade of honking cars quickly piled up behind it. The jeep liked the parade. Its horns were tubas blasting on VJ Day, its drivers veterans celebrating the war's end. The jeep thought Mr. Manlapit liked the parade too, because he was smiling, a thin smile that showed his teeth and made his face look

128

like a flower blooming. Death, though, did not like people celebrating. He twisted in his seat and yelled at the long line of cars,
"Hey, keep your pants on."

Higher and higher the jeep climbed as the road grew steeper
and steeper. "Hey, you sure this jeep isn't going to shake itself
apart." Stretch slapped the old man's knee. "Ha Ha!"

Mr. Manlapit pointed at a line of eucalyptus trees. "There,"
he said, and the jeep saw the pineapple fields give way to freshly
cut grass and white headstones. The trees whispered in the
wind, and the headstones looked like whitecaps on a stormy sea.
"Turn there," Mr. Manlapit said.

Stretch shook his head. "Not me. Cemeteries make me nervous."

Mr. Manlapit grabbed the steering wheel and forced the jeep
hard left, its wheels lifting off the ground, and when death
slammed on the brakes, the Jeep had to grab asphalt and gravel
to keep from smacking into a eucalyptus tree. It stopped an inch
from peeling bark.

"My boy is there," Mr. Manlapit said, pointing at the sea of
headstones. "My wife, too." The jeep wondered if the two lost
friends would suddenly appear. Thick grey clouds drifted across
the sky, promising rain. The jeep looked in its rear view mirror
and saw people dressed as if they had been to church, holding
clumps of white flowers and kneeling in front of headstones.
Engine idling, the jeep inhaled a huge gulp of eucalyptus smell
into his carburetor, and remembered Mr. Manlapit listening to
the mailman hiss, "Sorry. Sorry. Sorry." Red dust had blown
across from the cane field while his son's black dog howled and
snapped at the mailman's feet.

Now, sitting in the cemetery parking lot, the jeep tasted rust
and eucalyptus. Then it saw a shadowy figure rise from the
earth. And suddenly the jeep knew death was not this boy called

Stretch. Death had tricked them all. Death had been hiding, waiting for Mr. Manlapit to stop here. Run, the jeep wanted to yell, but it was only a jeep and did not have a voice. Mr. Manlapit sat with his chin resting in his hands, telling Stretch how after his son's funeral he had decided to sell his old jeep.

Run! the Jeep wanted to yell.

A huge drop of rain smacked into the windshield, and a shadowy black dog rose from the ground, barking.

Run!

"I am old," Mr. Manlapit said, drops of rain splashing through the hole in the jeep's canvas top. "I need someone to take care of my jeep."

A big, green 1965 Ford Fairlane, a huge overweight car, splashed out of the parking lot and headed down the road to Dream City. The jeep wanted to follow the Fairlane, wanted to fly over the pineapple fields, its radiator hissing hot steam, but Mr. Manlapit sat still, rain dripping on his knee.

"I'll make this jeep one of the family," Stretch said.

"First, I show you how to drive." Mr. Manlapit lifted one leg out of the jeep, slowly stepped onto the ground, lifted his other leg, slowly stepped into a puddle. Rain dripped down his cheeks as he rubbed the jeep's wet fender.

Death, inside a shadow running, rushed toward the jeep. Couldn't Mr. Manlapit see him?

"Buttah," Mr. Manlapit said, stepping to the driver's side of the jeep, "I love my jeep.

"Sure, big fella," Stretch said, and threw his leg over the stick shift, settled his bony butt into the worn springs of the passenger seat.

No, the Jeep wanted to scream, the old man can't see. You drive, Stretch.

Mr. Manlapit sat staring at the sea of headstones, thinking stick shift, clutch, gas! His hands gripped, warm and firm, the steering wheel, and his breath gently touched the windshield.

Now if only his foot would press the gas pedal

Death was running, waving as if he knew somebody in the jeep. Mr. Manlapit's foot edged toward the gas pedal. Death was so close, the jeep could smell him. He smelled of cane fields and fighting cocks. Gently, Mr. Manlapit's toe touched the gas pedal, and the jeep opened its gas lines, tightened its clutch, and jumped, rushed to ten, twenty, twenty-five miles per hour, straight out of the parking lot. Death leaped into the air.

Never had the jeep seen anything so scary. Now it knew why men feared death. Thirty. Thirty-three. Thirty-five miles per hour. The jeep was running for its life, twisting through sharp turns, wheels lifting off the ground, while Mr. Manlapit, looking straight ahead, revved the engine, and Stretch, face aflame with freckles, yelled, "Go, man. Go!"

Thirty-six. Thirty-seven. Thirty-eight. Thirty-nine. Dream city floated below them in a green sea of sugar cane, and from the sea the jeep felt ghosts rising. All around the jeep marched young soldiers. It heard Mr. Manlapit's fighting cocks, smelled Mrs. Manlapit's ginger perfume, saw the boy's pink lips kissing the old man's cheek. Forty miles an hour! The canvas top fluttered in the wind as the exhausted day faded from the sky. Stretch was flaming, Mr. Manlapit smiling, the wind a current blowing back their hair, and the clank clank clank of the jeep's little four cylinder engine was the sound of a boat battling a great sea of white flowers as big as army helmets. Forty-five miles an hour! The jeep looked in its rear-view mirror, and saw that death was wearing an army uniform. The black dog was running beside him, as a dog would run alongside a boy pulling a kite. And behind Patrick ran Colonel Blackman killed in the

Philippines, and Corporal Bracket who died in a car accident in his home town of Chicago, and Mrs. Manlapit whose heart had stopped beating in Dream City.

Wait, the jeep wanted to scream. Don't leave them. But Mr. Manlapit did not stop. He stared straight ahead, rain drops on his cheeks, foot on the gas pedal, fists turning white on the steering wheel, rushing toward Dream City. And seeing him, suddenly, the jeep felt like a man, wanted to scream. Go back. Go back! And most of all, it wanted to cry, but it could not cry, because it was only a jeep.

13. news crawling in hilo

You wake up screaming. The machine answers the phone.

"Professor, you there? This is Steamer. Remember, a student of yours? Very important question. A hypotheoretical question. Professor?"

You reach for the remote control. Slight pressure on the button produces a 27-inch video-image of a talking head above news crawl. Dengue fever cases reach 79. Welfare benefits cut. Attorney General seeks roundup of suspicious foreigners.

"Professor, here's my question. If I get hot looking at a woman who used to be a man, can that be love? Hypotheoretically, I mean. Or is it something twisted?"

You want to help this voice. It belongs, quite possibly, to a fellow human being, even if one prone to littering the world with disturbing phone messages. But love is not your specialty. Last night, it cost you $200 an hour. For an extra fifty, a young woman named Beatrice had stayed an extra hour to help with the remote control and chat about "Three's Company" reruns.

"Professor?"

She had moved quickly through the channels from "48 Hours" to "Three" CNN to "Three" to "60 Minutes" at exactly the right moment.

"Professor? Could you love a woman, I mean a man who has become a woman? Does that mean I'm gay?"

Razor-thin models reveal Victoria's Secrets above news crawl: Bush calls for return to normalcy. Time for Americans to stick together. The world has changed. Attorney General seeks roundup of suspicious foreigners.

You are not certain when your interest in the news became an addiction, when it became necessary to watch news even during the act of commercial sex. Perhaps, Beatrice would know. You could ask her how long ago she started earning the extra $50.

"Professor?"

Director of Homeland security warns, "Someone is trying to kill you."

***

How did you get from your apartment to the stern of Steamer's sampan? It's a mystery, but you are nearly awake, quite relaxed, and only vaguely in need of news crawl. Steamer points at the beach as the Sampan edges away from its anchor buoy. "Professor, the first time I saw her, she was walking on that beach. I wanted to shout something, anything, like one of those guys in the opera, singing crazy about love, but she looked too beautiful. Professor, what could a babe local girl see in me?"

This is a good question. If he was dressed as he is now— canvas shorts, frayed sweatshirt worn inside-out, with cheap, wraparound sunglasses—his chances of attracting a mate, even one who formerly possessed male genitalia, seemed to be limited. This is Hilo, and Hilo does not surrender its limited supply of daughters, cousins and nieces, transsexual or otherwise, to outsiders who dress like castaways and live on Sampans.

"I don't mean she's perfect," Steamer says. "She's got some crazy ideas, Professor."

You hear yourself asking, "The sex? Is it like being with...a woman?"

Steamer pushes hard on the tiller to avoid crashing into the Suisan dock. Now, the sampan is aimed at the breakwater. The horizon offers infinite blueness underlined by a blank space for news crawl.

"Well," he says, holding the tiller under his arm, "I don't know." He produces a misshapen joint that looks like a boa constrictor that has swallowed a pig, and lights the end with a red Zippo.

Steamer is a virgin? No wait. There are other possibilities.

"She says we have to sail around the world first, experience everything, and when we get back here, then we'll know we're in love and she'll sleep with me, and we'll live together forever." His coughing produces a cloud of industrial grade smoke, vaguely reminiscent of marijuana. "Do you think that's fair, Professor?"

He inhales deeply and then holds his breath. The boat rises and falls on the back of incoming swells.

"Sometimes," he says, "she lays her head against my chest and listens to my heart. We can stay like that for hours, feeling each other breathing. That's love, isn't it? I mean, hypotheoretically."

Memory moves at a sluggish crawl. It's coming back to you. Steamer is a carpenter, much favored by the local contractors who speak highly of his skills and pay little for them. To better himself he had enrolled in college, and despite erratic attendance and a tendency to answer all questions with metaphors pertaining to carpentry, such as blaming Freud for building a dream house without any drywall, he managed to reach his third year of studies in the philosophy department before he disappeared mysteriously Some said to work in the construction boom on the other side of the island. Others said to grow dope in Puna. Only recently had he reappeared, in possession of a decaying sampan and a girlfriend of questionable origins and appearance.

Was it already two years ago, when Steamer decided that his first assignment in your class was to write a 1500-word essay identifying the sexual subtext in King Kong? And a week after the deadline, he produced an odd poem scribbled on a faded chart of Hilo Harbor:

Nation with a four-hour erection
    by Steamer

In this new war, we're all soldiers.
Now go back to living normal lives.
Until its time to march in rank,
Remember, no one is safe.

We're all in uniform.
bearing tattoos of rank
Privates baring midriffs
lieutenants with pierced tongues
generals poised to administer corporal punishment
retribution, justice, wait, is that my cell phone?

Buy me an education,
DVD burn it in my brain
Got my handcuffs, whip,

S&M look, give me pain
with my sex. so I can do it again.

Sopranos pleasure. TV crime syndicate mob
Make me a survivor of Saddam's dismissal
It's only a flat-screen game.
Like, cool. Like hip. Like, high definition, ready to bleed.

Draft me into the all-volunteer army
March me in line to television time
Give me Janet Jackson Viagra gun.
Don't I look good in my Tom-Cruise flying machine?
talking on my GPS phone, dropping my ali mcbeal thin
bombs on Ophra's refugees?
American idol, reliving his beer-drinking youth,
Sober now, so kill America's most wanted, be home in time
for Fox news, god bless AA.

Proud to be in the front rank
Of high definition TV.
It'll be different, you'll see, on channel 33.
Honor, patriotism, justice
Radioactive ecstasy, on plasma scream

In this new war, we're x-box warriors, free to buy freedom
with free enterprise.
Broadcast da rappers, da gangstas
Let them take their jiggy to Baghdad streets
Drop that biological-weapon Pamala Anderson
To bitch-slap osama, the bachelor of Baghdad. Justifiable
Homicide

As long as they feel it, not me.
As I sit in front of my TV,
Watching King Kong
To relieve anticipated side effects.
THE END

At first, you had thought the poem a simple mistake. You attempted to correct Steamer, as you would have any other first-year student, by reminding him about the three lectures you had delivered on essay format and sticking to the subject assigned. He listened attentively, nodding his head at the right moments, and carefully noting the subject of his next assignment: To summarize the plots of *Voyage to the Center of the Earth* and *Some Like It Hot*. A week later he returned with three poems, one that almost made sense.:

Boys night out
    by Steamer

The geneticists made me bigger, stronger, smarter.
Now I search
the halls for dollies,
equally inspired,
selecting DNA samples with my tongue.

Money is worthless
the class war terminated
I walk among chimps
stealing their
inheritance
as they fall behind

I have a new heart, a bigger, faster brain,

so who will mate with me?
Our children will be
richer, smarter,
live forever,
free to travel space,
lifting upward
to find the secrets
of the universe.
THE END, pau.

<u>Born again! Clones</u>.
by Steamer

Doubling, doubling,
Over and over,
In search of life
Until
Born again! Clones,
Doubling, doubling,
Over and over,
in search of love,
Until...
Born again! Clones,
Doubling, doubling,
Over and over,
Searching out heaven.
St Peter at the pearly gate,
say, "Hey, wait. Who are you?
Two, four, six or eight?
Come back when you're"
Born again!
Clones,

doubling over and over again,
until it's too late,
for anything else
but double dates.
(All Pau)

Super Bowl 38DD
by Steamer

Fear the boob
Its coming for you

Fear the boob,
Its busting through,

Like the Hindenburg
Oh the humanity,

The grind, the hump,
Coming for you, Busting through,
Popping out from Viagra gloom

Fear the titty, da boob, da bust
What will the children think
Still remembering the taste
of mother's sweet milk?

Blitz it, tackle it, block it,
issue it a helmet and shoulder pads,
kick it through the goalposts
for sudden death overtime.
Penalize it for unsportsmanlike conduct,

and make it go back undercover,
where it belongs: half the distance to the goal.

***

"Professor?" A woman's voice calls from the cabin below. "Is that you?" A second later, Beatrice appears in tight shorts and a t-shirt. The old addiction takes hold.

Dengue fever victims reach 89. U.S forces poised to attack.

She places a radio in your lap, slides the dial to the all-news station, and sits across from you, with her arm around Steamer's neck. As the boat slides down a swell, she lets her leg drop to the side, revealing the edge of her black panties. Memory acts as a sluggish current, rich with the promise of tsunamis, hurricanes and perfumed secrets. You need the news.

"Tell him, professor. Tell him how it feels to be in love."

Steamer flicks the fat roach into the harbor and watches waves break over the jetty, waiting for you to say something. Along the horizon, radio news crawls lightly over the waves. Welfare rolls cut. President predicts new enemies. Director of homeland security warns.

"Love!" Steamer shouts at the horizon. "Goddamn, I need it!"

Someone is trying to kill you.

***

Beatrice has never been a student of yours. You have been very careful to avoid such entanglements, even ones based purely on commercial considerations. Beatrice was on campus only once, to have her transcripts evaluated and her portfolio analyzed for advanced placement. She presented you with a transcript from an Ivy League school and a tattered portfolio of photographs, a short story, and a poem. You remember now that you did not look at the name on the transcript, only at the

141

grade point average: 3.9 for five semesters of work in biology. The photographs were all black-and-white, all of naked women in churches. The short story was called "Black Umbrellas," the poem was about strippers:

Black Umbrellas
a story by Beatrice

It happens that you leave home and find yourself in a town where all the umbrellas are black. You are certain this is true because you have been in this city for three days and it has rained three times and every time it rains, black umbrellas bloom.

If you were at home, the first heavy drops of rain breaking against the window would cause blue and green umbrellas to pass in pools of red streetlight. Friends would call to meet for coffee or drinks. Instead, you are alone, walking along a broken strip of concrete across from a still bay, while being drawn along by a memory. You are reaching for the door to an art gallery when you hear a man's voice.

"I've had enough," he says, then the door swings open and he is facing you. He nods, looks at you, then up at the sky, shaking his head, but his hair does not move. It is black and cut extremely short. He is wearing a white shirt tucked into blue jeans and carrying a large black cardboard portfolio. You imagine it filled with photographs or drawings. With it tucked under his arm, he manages to find a cigarette and stick it between his lips.

"Can you help me?" he asks, handing you a book of matches.

You strike a match, and in the flickering light he appears cold and still, a statue in front of a votive candle. His skin is the white of a wedding gown. You remember him from earlier in the day, the professor who scrutinized your transcripts and writing sample. You sat in an uncomfortable chair while you waited for him to finish reading. He smelled of red wine and exercise.

Now, outside in the dark, raindrops begin to fall, and the professor says, "You look familiar."

Boredom and curiosity beg you to play a game. "We met to-day," you say. "I was thinking about going back to school. You changed my mind."

"I did? I didn't mean to." He holds the portfolio tightly under his arm, waiting for a response.

"It wasn't just you." You glance at the portfolio. "Anything good inside?"

"What?"

"In the gallery? The place you just walked out of. Anything good inside?"

"Nothing important. Pictures of waterfalls, plantation shacks, tourist stuff. I need a drink. You want a drink?"

Your high heels tap on concrete as you walk with him past a surf shop. Raindrops leave tiny black circles on the sleeves of your jacket. He tosses the cigarette into the gutter, says, "So, you're not a student?"

"Never was."

A police car passes with its lights flashing. You pass an old storefront with a light in the back, a yellow light behind drawn curtains. A dog barks in a vacant lot. You remember the smell of cigarettes and perfume.

"I don't drink with students," he says. "It's a small town. Everybody knows everybody."

"I don't know you."

He takes your hand, leads you into a Mexican restaurant with concrete floors. Sombreros and back velvet paintings are nailed to the wall, ragged piñatas hanging from the moldy ceiling. You sit at a table near the door, so you can see and smell the bay.

He's forty, maybe fifty. It's hard to tell. Your lips are painted bright red to make them appear fuller than they are. And your skin is hidden under thick white make-up. Punk-kabuki. You sit with your back straight, a cheap charm bracelet on your wrist, with tiny silver surfers dangling

The waitress brings him a margarita on the rocks without salt. "What would you like, honey?" she asks.

"The same."

Will he tell you what is inside the portfolio? He has placed it on the table, within your reach. You are certain you know what's inside. Pictures, photographs of moody women with harden bodies stretched out in window light. You're curious. That's all.

"Tell me more about the school thing," he asks.

"I need a drink before I tell stories."

He laughs, raises his glass to you. "Good answer."

"I bet you say that to all your students."

The waitress leaves a bucket glass on your table without bothering to stop. You can smell the tequila. It tastes even stronger. You settle your chin in the palm of your hand, your elbow next to the empty glass, as the surfers ride imaginary waves.

You say, "In this fantasy I have, we meet in the street and he takes me to his room. He doesn't ask my name. And I don't want to know him. I only want him that one time. Maybe I will hurt him. Just enough to make him wonder." You drink the rest of your margarita. It is smooth and strong. "And if he wants me enough, and touches me just right, so good I can stand life another day, maybe then I'll give him what he wants."

His fingertips tighten on the margarita glass.

"How about you? What do you want, Professor?"

"I want to look at you."

You follow him up two flights of stairs. His room is at the middle of the hall. He turns on the light, leaves the portfolio next to the door, and goes into the bathroom. You turn off the light, look out the window while you undress. You can see the entrance to his building. A man and woman stop on the sidewalk. There is a streetlight above them. They talk for a moment.

He turns and walks away. The woman watches him for a moment, calls something, waves, then hurries in the other direction.

You hear the bathroom door open. He sits on the bed. You take chair across from him. You are wearing yellow panties and a red bra. You let your head fall back. The light from the window touches your neck, falls between your breasts, settles on your thigh. He cannot reach you. You move your hands between her thighs, touch yourself.

He kneels. You can smell the cigarette smoke in his hair "Please, " he says.

His lips touch your silk panties.

***

Later, while he sleeps, you dress in the shadows. In the light from the window, you open the portfolio. He has used the same model for the all the photographs. She is thin, with short black hair, small breasts, and pale skin. His much type.

Only three interest you. In the first, delicate shadows fall from stained glass windows onto the shoulders of the woman kneeling naked before an altar, her arms outstretched. Candles flickering.

In the second, she kneels among neatly dressed people at the communion rail, her mouth open for the Eucharist. You are almost certain you can hear the starched movement of the priest's vestments, smell the wine on his breath as he settles the host on her tongue Off to the side, the same woman sits in a confessional. The light falls on her legs. They are long and white and lead to a shadow between her thighs.

In the last photograph, a woman is silhouetted against the bright light of a church's entryway. Past her naked shoulder, you see the rooftops of a small town. Rain falls as bright sunlight seeps through dark clouds.

You leave the other photographs at the foot of the bed, snap the portfolio shut, and hurry down the stairs. You stop under the streetlight and look up at his dark window. To stop the rain you hold the portfolio over your head. A young man brushes past you in canvas shorts and a torn t-shirt, muttering about love. The rain falls harder, and his black umbrella blooms.

The End.

A Poem: Postmodern Aloha-stress Syndrome
Or: Contemplating the statue in front of the Hawaii
Convention Center, from the doorway of Club Rocks-ya
by Beatrice

Try listen. Can't you hear them rockin?
Naked women, come and go, talking of dollar bills
and Michelanglo.
Evil bass, heavy drum, witchy women, in a Viagra gloom
urging me to confess.

Brass, sculptured cuz, Pacific David, kneeling still,
It was me that poured the cement. Stole your soul.
Planted you for the tourists gaze.

No more lines, only paragraphs in revolt
screw conformity

At night, while the city slept in its Halloween stupor of Christmas cheer and queer fear, I de-revolutionized in gossamer underwear (Kalvin da Kine). Ala Moana shopping bag instead of ski mask to hide my face (no shame), I borrowed into the warehouse of discontent. Past discontinued, price-rolledback merchandise, I charged, visa-man in Bank of Hawaii slacks and

Patrick Henry aloha shirt, whispering "Give me Liberty House or give me nordstrum...or a raincheck. Five percent off my next purchase.

So much a part of the downtown density in the downtown uniform, so locals only, I avoided detection, assimilation, acculturation, incarceration, as I robbed the book of its last line.

Try listen. Can't you hear them rocking? On the other side of my workers-comp, unemployment-check, student-loan door, the women come and go, talkin whorey, offering snatch and crack, the colonel's finger lickin good, frisky or original, for a buck. Their customers come and go, bowing low, to avoid the gaze of your bronze sea.

Can't you hear them? They want to steal it back. Steal my GTE stock , repossess my illegitimate dream, trade my HMSA for quest, rip a hole in my Mahalo Air. Is this paranoia taking its toll, its 10.5 excise tax? A hundred yen for a pound of flesh? Or is it a downturn in the market, a minor adjustment, a deficit turned surplus, turned deficit. A shift from fee-simple to grease hold? A banker's thumb up my yakazuya? Or is wealth truly about to shift from the shifty to the shiftier, from the rich to the richer, away from the genetically repossessed?

Should I sell my ten-pound bag of calrose? trade it for IBMpunahoamericakaonline? Beg them to wire me, network me, ethernet me, fax me, e-mail me, care of prison@hawaii.edu? Or should I flee the scene at the wheel of my car payments? Avoid a mom-and-pop meltdown in an empire of shaved batu, board a not-so-pleasant holiday slingshot aimed at sam boyd? Deedee hi-low and away we blow. Ecstasy!

Perhaps if I surrender peacefully (shaka brah), they'll make me a trustee of the longhorn state. Strictly legal, reconditioned, remodeled, re-educated, I will repent. My feet in concrete, my slippahs behind bars, a new foundation for a deconstructed estate, I will wave my little red safeway card, Mao say two-for-five. Buy one busted dream, get one free.

Cuz, malo david in bronze, you should make the same deal: memories in exchange for respectability, identity for a mortgage in the termite's second city, cracked soul for a taste of Club rocksya's cracked seed.

Can't you hear them rockin? The women come and go. The governor, the mayors, the senators, the police chiefs, here they come, opening day. Bronze cuz, hide your thin roll of dollar bills. Pay your rent. Sell your blood for five cents a quart, your eggs for five grand, your sperm for a buck. Fake content. Dig a hole, in a subterranean hideaway, rich with the smell of manoa valley retirement checks.

And if the builders find you, hoping to flatten the rough edges, make you part of the game, part of the sidewalk, part of the aloha, disguise yourself as a prostitute or politician, and model walk—in front of the conventional center. Mimic the sacred dance, hula in high heels, Bangkok style, with a hint of victoria's secrets and a splash of vegas thrown in for sense of place. Lift you skirt so everyone can see culture under glass.

Make your self a warrior. Wear an ice-head H. Stay up with the joneses. Be the new savior, one t-shirt, one new hat, new chant. No longer a rainbow in the big brother real world we wear paper rubbers in sexual traffic jams inspired by millionaires too cheap, too scared, too needy, too tired, too cellular, too digitalized, two for the price of one.

Bronze pourer of earthly grace, driven deaf by the jukebox echo of real estate, real estate, real estate, can't you her them rockin, cuz? Feel their sticky green next to your crotch. Unoriginal sin, that's life, that's strife, rife with the copper penny taste of char siu bullets shot from video game guns. Virtual mana held prisoner in bronze.

The End, Beatrice.

***

You are the professor. The girl and Steamer are gone. Two writers at sea. With your back to the Tsunami Museum, you watch their Sampan drift to sea, pushed along by the flat surface of increasing humidity, the memory of her skin, the touch of her fingers on the edge of your desire. How you got to this street corner that smells of mildew and the passage of time is a mystery.

You are alone, in town, on a street facing the bay. Steamer's sampan crosses a sliver of moonlight. From the look of the ocean, if he manages to sail beyond the jetty, his boat will be torn to pieces by waves of terrorists, cross currents of CIA, tidal waves of religious desire.

You press your ear to the museum's rough concrete wall, listening for her heartbeat. Instead you hear a fading memory of her voice.

In search of the latest news, you follow a damp sidewalk past empty storefronts with taped windows. Hand-painted signs announce the last days of a going-out-of-business sale. In the dim light of a stairwell, a man and woman huddle around cartoons of Chinese takeout. They smile as if they know you, and then go back to scooping up beef broccoli with chopsticks.

At Pestos, a couple holds hands across a table topped with seared ahi salad and Mehana beer. You tap the glass, wanting to ask what love feels like, but when they look up, a tickertape warning appears: Dengue Fever cases reach 99. President predicts biological terrorism.

Next door, Reuben's is exploding with lights and laughter and trays of corn chips and super-strength salsa washed down with margaritas powered by double doses of tequila. Loud talk reaches from the back of the restaurant to the street, where you are standing, waiting for the news that will change everything.

14. fingertip chat

Monday

: Last night, I searched for you.

: Don't. You promised.

: Not that kind of search. I closed my eyes and tried to imagine you in my arms.

: A fantasy? Is that what you want?

: No. A dream.

: What's the difference?

: A fantasy is like one of those letters in a girlie magazine, scripted from beginning to end. A dream is unpredictable, nothing certain, with no beginning or end, like a   storm.

: And in this storm, what am I wearing?

: Last time I looked, nothing.

Tuesday

: Have you been dreaming?

: I'm not certain. It was late. I closed my eyes and tried to imagine you lying in bed. The next thing I know, I was climbing up the mountain, on a muddy path that   zigzagged through a cow pasture, heading for a stone cottage with a tin roof.

: You have pastures in Hawaii?

: Not like this one. Wild horses were running through the mist, and thick black clouds were rushing across the sky, away from an old town, where the buildings were made of wood, and sagging, and everything was dark, except for a bright neon sign that kept blinking: Warning! Floods, tsunamis, hurricanes, earthquakes, and lava flows.

: Sounds like a nightmare.

: No. It felt dreamy and smooth and promising, and when the door to the cottage opened, I found you lying in bed, under a thick comforter, in a room with a brick fireplace.

: Did you touch me?

: I wanted to but when I stepped toward you, some
thing strange happened.

: Tell me.

: I smelled coffee, fried eggs, Tabasco, and Portuguese sausage.

: Portuguese sausage?

: It's like pepperoni, only bigger and better. When I was kid my father made it for breakfast every morning, and when the smell drifted up to my room, I knew it was time to wake up.

: So I remind you of Portuguese sausage and Tabasco?

: And when I try to touch you, I wake up.

Wednesday

: I wish I could dream about Hawaii. In my dreams, it never rains. The world is flat and I live in a trailer behind a diner next to a highway that runs through a desert. In the morning I wake up to the sound of a dishwasher and a cook banging pots and pans, and trucks going so fast, they make the walls shake.

: You're a drifter.

: Used to be, not anymore. I've come home and I can never leave. This is my mother's place and I'm here to help her. She loves the desert. Every morning, she sits in front of a stack of pancakes oozing Mrs. Butterworth and watches the sunrise turn the desert purple. Luis Ruiz is crooning on the radio, and the earth is moving, spinning around the sun, but when I touch my mother's shoulder, everything goes still.

: That's when I walk in.

: Wearing cowboy boots and tight Jeans.

: No shirt?

: I didn't look.

Thursday:

: In your dream, what color is my hair?

: It keeps changing.

: My skin?

: One day you're black, one day white. Lately you've been, kinda Japanese light brownish, maybe Indian.

: I'm programmable.

: You uncontrollable. You flicker and change. Short and tall, big and small, black and white, blond, redhead, brunette.

: Am I young or old?

: You're everything I've ever wanted.

Friday

: Fridays are good.

: Friday nights I like to party, over to the diner. Have a few beers. People come in from down the road, mostly old timers, but young people too. We listen to music and drink beer and dance some.

: I go to the harbor, to drink beer. If I'm lucky a cruise ship will be docked with all its lights on and a jet will fly across the moon. Tourists will fall out, like shooting stars, or big fat raindrops, singing "Welcome to paradise!" Then I'll walk home through town, and the college kids will be at the bar and Jimmy, the guy who owns the surf shop will be sitting in the back with his wife and kids eating chow fun noodles from a white carton.

: What will you be wearing?

: Jeans and rubber slippahs.

: Aren't Fridays special where you live?

: Tight jeans and cowboy boots.

: That's better.

Saturday

: Saturday nights suck.

: I could live single for the rest of my life if it weren't for Saturday nights.

: I get so lonely I drink shots of Jim Beam and listen to the Cowboy Junkies.

: I get so lonely I sit naked in the bathroom and drink Budweiser.

: Why the bathroom?

: With the window closed and a towel stuffed under the door, the shower and sink turned to full blast hot create a good steam bath.

: That's lonely.

: It gets more worse. When I run out of hot water, I stand in front of the mirror and put my hand on the glass to feel another person.

: How do glass people feel?

: Just out of reach.

Sunday

: Do you believe in god?

: Every time I fly in an airplane.

: Don't kid me.

: I'm not. While the plane is on the ground, I thank god for everything.

: What's everything? Your steam baths?

: I thank him for the way the town smells, even if it is moldy. The way the breeze blows off the ocean after a humid day. I thank him for me knowing the name of every person in town. I thank him for the rain, the tomorrow, the past.

: Do you thank him for Internet chat?

: For that, too. Then as the plane leaves the ground, I start begging. "Jesus, Mary, and Buddha. And anybody I missed. Confucius, Muhammad Ali, please keep this flaming tube of flimsy steel from crashing into the sea."

: Last night I searched for you.

: Is it my turn to say that we promised not to do that?

: I closed my eyes and tried to imagine you in my arms. Instead, I found myself sailing across a desert that became an ocean. I was pulling myself along by the stars, searching for you.

: Did you find me?

: After the storm, a dreamy storm that tossed me onto an island, I woke up under a thick comforter. Rain was pounding on a tin roof, and I felt you standing next to me in the dark. I felt your breath on my cheek, on my lips.

: Did I touch you?

: Close your eyes. Move your fingertips softly over the keys. Do you feel the space between the keys? Do you feel me?

sunday

15. working for jesus

Yesterday, Jesus whispered in my ear. "I need a favor. Go find Noelie and kiss her until she turns on her Christmas lights."

None of it made sense to me. But Jesus, he said, "See, I'm too busy to do a job my father ordered me to do, and the old man has a temper. I've seen him kick a couple out of paradise for eating a piece of fruit, so you know what I mean. I don't want to end up crucified. You do this for me, I'll owe you one." Then he shoved me into the street.

I would have been killed. Believe me, I heard the bus and felt the rush of cars. But a baritone who stunk of stale beer and rotten sardines grabbed my arm. "Going my way?" he sang, as he jerked me back to the sidewalk.

Clickity-clack, clickity-clack. I heard the busted wheel of a shopping cart.

"Forty days and forty night, I've wandered this concrete desert, my blind brother," he sang, slightly off pitch. "Merry Christmas. Doing the work of Jesus."

Clickity-clack.

He led me along the bank of a river, swirling with moped noise, to a concrete valley, or was it an alley, where the tired chords of "Witchy Woman" rode gusts of air-conditioning laced with opium perfume (imitation, much sweeter than the original), as my guide warned me, "Be joyful, my son. We walk among the women of mercy."

Spiked heels—tip-tap, tip-tap—announced the arrival of a soprano. "It ain't easy," she sang, "being a working girl."

"Me," said ckickity-clack. "I'm working for Jesus."

"No kiddin. He let you work for him smelling like dead fish?"

"Jesus, he don't care about smell. He's the fisher of men."

"Lucky for you. That shopping cart belong to Jesus? Jesus own Safeway? What you doing wearing a Santa Claus outfit and carrying all that dog food in Jesus's shopping cart?"

"Jesus, he got a plan."

"What about you, sailor?" she sang in my ear. "You make much money playing blind?"

"He don't talk much. He's a prophet."

"How can he be a prophet and not talk much?"

"Jesus he works in all kine ways."

"That right, honey?"

Finger tips brushed my cheek.

"You're kinda cute. You like brunettes, honey?"

"He can't see no brunettes."

"I got this friend. Just up the street. She'd be perfect for you, honey."

"He's working for Jesus. He can't be foolin wit sex."

"This ain't about sex."

"What it about?"

"This is about—"

Her thinking sounded like a traffic jam on a rainy street.

"This is about comforting the needy."

"About healing?"

"That's right, Santa. About healing the sick."

"Make way." Clickity-clack. "Coming through. Doing the work of Jesus."

"Whadevahs." Tip-tap.

They led me through darkness, to a step up, from slippery concrete, to a creaky iron gate. "Before you go inside," tip-tap said, "I have to warn you. My friend likes to talk."

"She speaks in tongues!" Clickty-clack.

"Mostly in English."

"The voice of demons!"

"Yeah, sure." Tip-tap. "She's had her demons. Ain't we all?" She nudged me forward. "This place used to be lit up with Christmas lights. Thousands of them. Noelie kept them burning all year round. Only 69¢ a day, she'd say, and look at how much beauty they bring. That's what she'd say. Now she's in the dumps. The lights they been off for weeks."

"Blind man, he goin to cast out demons."

Her hand brushed over my wallet and settled in the small of my back. "Honey, you don't forget to pay. You be nice. No need to worry. Just sit and listen. In the end, you'll both feel better." A screen door creaked open. "Noelie," she called, pushing me inside, into the pitter-patter of delicate feet.

"Dear, dear," a soft voice cooed. "Who do we have here?" She smelled of cookies, chocolate chip. "I'm glad you came by. I was so lonely that I was talking to myself." She sat me on a puffy couch. "Do you ever do that, dear? Talk to yourself? Would you like some tea?" She pitter-pattered away. I heard water running, a teapot clank on the stove.

"They say only crazy people talk to themselves." Her voice arrived from far away. "But I'm not crazy, I just like to talk." Pitter-patter. "You're lucky," she whispered in my ear, "being blind. You know why? All the time I see things I don't want to see." Her words, a Kona storm, swirled around me, tearing the tin roof off my abandoned home. "I'm small but I'm strong." She sat next to me. "Feel my muscle." Her foot settled in my lap. "No, silly, not there. Here, in my thigh."

The teapot whistled.

"Wait." Pitter-patter. The whistling stopped. Pitter-patter. "Here, I'm back." Slowly, carefully, gently, she settled into my lap. "I don't want to see," she said. "Not anymore." Her breath touched my lips. "I wish everything would go away. Not you. I want you to stay."

"Noelie," the soprano called from outside. "You okay?"

Gently, she shifted her weight. "It's scary out there," she whispered.

Outside, a thousand noises streamed. Sidewalks crackled with cell-phone pleas. Passing cars spilled fragmented laughter onto broken bones.

"He's out there," she whispered over the clamor of barking dogs. "Santa Claus. Trying to stay alive in that world of crap."

Clickity-clack.

"You know what I want for Christmas." She placed my hands on her waist, moved them slowly to her silk-covered breasts. "You know what I want for Christmas?" I felt her body stretch against my belly. Her lips touched my chin. Currents of her sound swirled around me, like a lover's arms. She kissed me gently on the cheek.

In that instant, I saw her house covered with Christmas lights. Thousands of them crawled like mysterious vines through nativity scenes. They surrounded three wise men on the porch, reached ten huge candles on the windowsills, and on the walls covered a hundred elves. They climbed up the branches of a neon Christmas tree to a giant Star of David perched on the roof. Then they blinked out, all of them dead.

She kissed my lips, until the lights began to flicker. I kissed her. Not a peck, but the Frenchie kind. The living room exploded, pink and green. The roof blew off and the clouds broke open. I kissed her again. Her lips ignited a multi-colored nebula. Old friends wearing wings swirled in a fluid sky, playing ukuleles, eating thick spam sandwiches and drinking frosty beers from icy coolers. We gazed in wonder, as a big black Santa Claus at the helm of a shopping-cart sleigh pulled by thirteen mangy poi dogs lifted off the ground. Riding inside, a red-haired babe in high heels waved to Noelie and sang soprano. "Honey, we're going home. No more sorrow, no more pain." Tip-tap.

The dogs barked and strained. The sleigh swooped through the door, the babe grabbed Noelie and tossed her in. What could I do? I watched the three of them rise into the sky.

They flew upward, leading an endless line of people, everyone who had died since the beginning of time, no matter how, in wars, in the electric chair, in plagues, in shootings, in bed with guilty lovers, no matter, as the soprano babe and Noelie sang, "Going home, to a better place. No more sorrow, no more gun, no more thirst, no more hatred, no more sorrow!" Tip-tap. Pitter-patter.

"Praise the heavens," shouted Santa Claus. "Praise Vishnu, Buddha, Lono and all the rest. They made the blind man see." Clickity Clack.

"Pure joy!" Noelie sang, looking frizzed out and stylish in clingy celestial pink. "Pure love," she sang. "Pure peace."

Clickity-clack, tip-tap, pitter-patter.

16. why i live in a tsunami zone

for three weeks the family searched for the diary and turned up nada. Me, I closed my eyes, tapped my rubber slippers together, and woke up Hilo. Three hours later, under a black umbrella, I was flipping through the rain-spotted pages.

First entry: Sept. 1, 1998
The taxi driver's fingers caress a dog's head in the shape of an umbrella handle. Its ruby eye stares at my chest. Can it see what I am?
***

I had heard stories about Hilo, so I bought an extra-large umbrella at the Wiki-Waki store. Good thing, too, because the second I stepped onto the sidewalk across from the harbor, a rain drop the size of a softball smacked me in the eye. Knocked me dizzy. Funny thing, though, when I popped open my umbrella, right away I was a marked man. The mob of squeakers playing soccer, knee-deep in mud, froze in mid-kick. Startled, their parents glanced first at the ocean then turned suspicious eyes on me. Even the traffic cop in the Cushman stopped to ask, "Are you lost?"

Entry 2: Sept. 21, 1998

The loneliness comes in waves, sweet blue waves filled with memories. Then it folds, breaks into a thousand pieces, and covers me in Hilo rain. During these stolen moments, this escape from headlines, from his voice and eye begging me, the children below sneak through buffalo grass, on a forbidden path to a freezing pond. Their laughter rises in a splendid dance.

***

I looked up, expecting to see a thick black cloud. Nothing, just clear blue skies. The cop in the Cushman thought I was looking at the thick red line on the cafe window. "Tidal wave," he said, lifting his chin proudly. "Twenty people died in that one." As I stretched, on tiptoes, to touch the heavy brushstroke, a blurry cloud of reflected Harley Davidson flew underneath my armpit. The XXL wahine squeezed onto the back of the black-and-blue Local Boy held a suitcase under one arm and two umbrellas under the other. Her deep-throated laughter disappeared in a wave of twin-V roar.

Entry 3, Sept 25, 1998

The windows open onto a point of land covered with Banyan trees, Elephant Ear, Ironwood, and Cook Pine. The kids call them Christmas trees. In the morning I wake to sounds of birds and motorcycles. The air smells vaguely of lead. In bed I feel my body lifting upward, all weight gone in the joy of the sunrise. Over the giant Banyan tree, the volcano appears, burned red by the sun, as neighbors back into parking spaces pointed at the evacuation route.

***

Past the expensive noodle place, the sad old Kress building, and behind the Tsunami Museum, I climbed metal stairs and squinted through the dirty window stenciled with William Peach Real Estate. Billy was sitting at a steel desk in the dim light of a 40-watt bulb, leafing through a pile of papers. The second he saw me, he stashed them in the top drawer.

"What's with the black umbrella?" he asked, sticking his head out the door.

"It's raining."

"You call this rain?"

The plastic face of my 10-buck Timex was fogged over and covered with raindrops. "Get in," he said, motioning me toward shadows. While I shook the water off my umbrella, he watched the street. Once we were inside, he locked the door and pulled down the curtain. Billie was a prime example of how far a guy can go on a high-priced education and a rabid case of paranoia. I laid the photograph on the desk, next to an opened bottle of Jim Beam. "You know the face?"

"Sure," he said. "I know the face. I called you, right? It's all business with you. No hello. No talk story. No nothing."

"The family's worried."

"About their reputation?"

"Their son has disappeared."

"Their son's dead. You know it, they know it. What they want is the diary, right?"

Like I said, too many Oliver Stone movies. He poured a shot of whiskey into a paper cup. "Remember the night you almost drowned?" he asked, his face half outside the circle of a dim 40-watt bulb.

The lighter-fluid smell of Jimmy Beam made me taste a memory of Kahului Harbor. Ahhh, diesel fuel and raw sewage.

But the photograph in Billy's hand had the unmistakable look of an IOU. "Drowning is not a nice way to die," he said.

"No way is nice."

Entry 4, Sept. 30, 1998

I find my memory in the freezing pond. Fed from deep within the volcano, the pond is clear, fresh, and icy cold. Not even the kids can stand the cold. They leap in, surface in a rush, and scramble up the jagged lava rocks. My toes touch the freezing glass. I can see the rocks below as if I am looking into an aquarium glass. I dive flat, feel the cold pierce my heart. It takes me 20 seconds to swim across, in water so deep my hands never touch bottom. On the way back, I stop to catch my breath. The children cry, "How deep is it? How deep?" I exhale and let myself sink. My feet touch the silky bottom, but my arms cannot reach the surface. When I look up, I see memories.
***

When Billy went looking for his keys in the back room, I checked the drawer. The rental agreement on top warned that the undersigned were acknowledging that they were aware of the danger of living in Keaukaha, a tsunami zone. Other threats included drought, earthquakes, floods, forest fires, high surf, high winds, hurricanes, landslides, thunderstorms, tornadoes, tropical storms, volcanic eruption and water spouts.

KEAUKAHA the form said in bold print may also be subject to technological disaster: accidental missile launch, dam rupture, explosions, hazardous material spills, pollution (air oil water), transportation disruption, and utility failures. Civil disturbance, health epidemics and infestation, resource shortages, and terrorism.

Hell, I was thinking, what would a terrorist want in Hilo? Then I caught a glimpse of a pink flier under the lease. Something to do with a rally on election day. In the margin Billy had
168

scribbled Hilo is wet streets, unemployment lines, food stamps, abandoned houses, failed businesses, drug deals, empty hotels. Escape is useless. But the rent is cheap.

Then he appeared, keys in hand, umbrella under his arm.

"Where we headed?" I asked, following him to the door.

"Keaukaha."

Entry 5: Nov. 1, 1998

Why do I live in a tsunami zone? Today is hot and sunny. Three teenage girls are the only ones at the pond. I walk to the second pond and lie in the sun smelling their suntan oil and listening to them chatter. They will soon be women. Are these girls the descendants of kings and queens? The girls shake out their long black hair and I feel god in me. Behind them, a group of teenage boys appear, transfixed by the beauty of the girls. They smile, and one grabs his crotch. "Bumby," he smiles. "They get raped." Their laughter settles like a shadow.

***

We drove past the airport and kept going, past the Harley Davidson shop, the tourist ship, the refinery, the sewage plant. The air was thick with salt and humidity. When we passed the fourth evacuation-route sign, I asked, "Do you guys really get tidal waves?"

"Twenty in the last sixty years."

"Who the hell lives out here?"

"Mostly Hawaiians. On Hawaiian Home Lands."

That made sense. We passed another tiny blue sign that announced an evacuation route. "Forget those," Billie said. "The route dead-ends 25 yards inland. You're better off on foot, running."

"You can outrun a tidal wave?"

"Hell, no. You crazy?"

169

Entry 6: Nov. 2

A storm rages the surf is up, the pool is gone, the salt water breaks strong and furious over the lava rock. The freezing pond is murky. The tree roots are hidden below the water. I feel the earth shake every time a wave breaks. I lie at the edge of the storm, feeling the wind race across my face, the power of the ocean coming for me. The memories will not leave me. In the storm I see Joey's lips.

***

The girls are waiting for us. Local girls, dark, real beauties, hiding under baggy shorts and over-sized t-shirts. They won't talk to me, but Billie goes over and they're all smiles. One of them points at a clump of trees, tall pines that look out of place perched on volcanic rock. Billie and me we poke around in the crevices for a couple of minutes and find the diary wrapped in plastic.

Entry 7: Nov. 3.

At the polling place the people in line hug and kiss, exchange stories of lost friends. Around me the bodies swirl in rekindled friendship. Alone I stand with my memories. While two Hawaiian women check the list for my name, I see the killer, his mouth a jagged hole, throwing stones at Joey to keep him from reaching shore. I am too frightened to move. Instead of a woman's voice saying, "Sign there." I hear, "Suck that, faggot!"

***

Billy and I sat at the edge of the pond. My job was to destroy the diary. No doubt Billy wanted me to turn it over to the police or newspapers, to do something, anything. Billie didn't know much about the world. He hadn't learned a thing from the last

170

election. Me, I figured dead voices were just more trouble. Better to keep those memories in the closet. I edged closer to the pond, stuck my big toe in the water. Christ, it was freezing. The girls were sitting on pink towels. I looked up, and a raindrop hit me in the eye. Then it poured, and Billy ran, but the girls didn't flinch. Their umbrellas bloomed bright orange with pink flowers. The oddest sight I had ever seen, those girls with orange umbrellas at the edge of a freezing pond, chatting in the Hilo rain. I popped open my umbrella, but too late. When I looked at the diary, the last page was spattered with rain, the words already dripping down the page, almost gone.

Nov. 3
The surf's strong today. If death comes for me, my soul will remain in this pond.

Writer's Note:
This story is based on a news report from Maui that detailed the death of a man in the ocean off Kahului. The victim was beaten and chased into the water late at night and kept from returning to shore by two men who threw stones at him and threatened to kill him if he returned to shore, until he tired and drowned in the surf.

17. remembering black

granite

Wailuku--The traveling exhibit of the Vietnam Veterans Memorial arrives in Kahului tomorrow. The life-size representation of the Washington, D.C, monument will be on display in the lot adjacent to the MEO offices from 9 a.m. to 9 p.m.

***

David, do you remember me? I look older, sure. Twenty-five years older. I still got some of my hair, most of it, anyway. Enough for a jar-head cut like yours. A woman I know tells me that my face looks tired. I tell her it's the sun. The sun has burned the hell out of me. You'd like it here, David. There's warm water, good waves, and plenty of fish and lobster. There'll be surf tomorrow. I can hear it building.

Can you see me? Hell, after what I did, I wouldn't blame you for never wanting to see me, not here, not like this, not anywhere. Me, I got a job, a bed, sometimes a woman, and you, you got to be a memory.

Everyone is proud of you. That's what you got, David. They're proud of you.

People come to your wall, they treat it like church. The first time I went to see you, there were hundreds of people waiting in line to pass along the granite. There were old women dressed like my mother, like when she went to church, and young kids, and men in civilian clothes but wearing jungle boots or airborne insignia or field jackets. More than one of them was kneeling down and crying and leaving things, flowers, a pint of whiskey, pictures, lots of high school graduation pictures and Marine Corp stuff.

This wall is the wrong place for you. You never went to church. Heck, though, even in Washington, with all those other monuments, you'll be close to the water. Guys surf this harbor. The water is never clear, and when the wind is blowing, the air smells of sewage, and the pineapple cannery, and diesel fuel. That's the smell of Maui's economic opportunity. But on the right swell, we get waves.

They should bring you to Baldwin Park. Right now, the county workers would be grilling teriyaki meat. They'd be waving their hands over the coals to fan the fire, and there'd be kids surfing, and Hawaiian music from radios. The water is clear out there, and there's a good reef break. You'd feel at home.

I guess it's good the real wall is in Washington, close to all the rest of the monuments for dead soldiers. Now, you're right around the corner from the Increments. It's a housing tract like we grew up in. You know, ranch style with carports and lawns and too many cars so people have to park on the grass or in the street. It's better where you're at, right. I stay in the country, mostly. I rent a house past Waihee and my neighbors they grow taro, papaya and banana. There's a stream in the valley, ginger and bamboo, too. And down the road a rocky point good for spear fishing. You'd like that.

I got a job working for a newspaper. Most often, I'm the sports guy but when they got something that no one else wants to cover, they send me. The other day they sent me to Kihei, that's a resort sprawl on the other side of the island, to find out if the tourists were right to be complaining about cane smoke. The plantation burns it here to make harvesting the cane easier and cheaper. Most of it gets blown toward Kihei, and everyone knows its bad but the sugar people got to live too, right. Anyway, I was driving down the center of the island between the two volcanoes, and I hit a patch of smoke, then a clearing, then a cane fire that must've been a mile long, straight down to the sea. The cane cutters were in there, a line of women in red scarves, red flames rising to the sky, feeding a black mushroom cloud. My eyes were watering; the cane smoke was so thick I couldn't breathe.

So I drove to the nearest resort and sat at the poolside bar drinking margaritas until the sun went down. They got a beautiful sunset over there, and I was lucky enough to have a clear night, so I could watch the navy bomb the hell out of Kahoolawe. The parachute flares were pouring orange light on the dry hills, and when the bombs hit, I felt the explosions in my feet even though that island was ten miles away. The Navy sure knows how to kill kiawe trees and goats. And people.

Remember the night we got so drunk we tried five different kinds of cigars? Wasted. You stripped and ran into the street chasing that VW full of girls. We did some crazy things. You're a hero now, but you know we did crazy things. We were drunk and it was the end of the summer, and we were through working in the fields, through with everything, so it doesn't matter.

Maybe I'm still crazy. That's my problem, that's what people say. I got my mother's blue eyes and my father's brown skin, but I didn't get either one's brains. Maybe that's why I'm here, and you're a hero. You were always the smart one, without even trying. You were on the swim team. You worked and saved for the VW. You lifted weights. You were big and tall and strong and the babes liked you. Me, I was always small. You wore black rubber slippers. I wore blue. All the time. Flip-flop, flip-flop. Like the two of us were already in Hawaii. That was the plan, right, David? We were supposed to go to Hawaii, remember?

You cut your hair flat on top. I wanted mine long.

What else could you do? A guy's got to satisfy his parents and himself, right? We weren't so different, were we? We both wanted out.

You'd like the sunrise on Haleakala. We could stand at the rim of the volcano, ten thousand feet up, and watch the sky turn red. Remember the time we drove up the mountains to get snow? The heater in your VW didn't work, and I had to drive because your hands were too cold. You found a pair of gym socks under the seat and used them for gloves. We were drinking Christian Brothers brandy to stay warm, and the radio was making screeching sounds, like maybe somewhere behind all that static was music. The wind was blowing so hard the car kept sliding across the centerline.

We surfed some big waves that last summer. You were brave, right? No scaring you. You never could surf as good as me. I was the surfer. Don't get me wrong. You were tough. And you were the better abalone diver. You knew all the good spots. Me, I never could hold my breath long enough. But I was the better surfer and I could drink more too. Remember how we left your car in the sand, you said if your father wanted it he could dig it out, and we walked to Dafun's house. We left our slippers by the door, local style, and drank the hell out of the lifeguard punch, the stuff in the plastic cooler. Remember that? Red wine and pineapple juice, vodka, rum, beer for bubbles, with orange slices and a ten-pound block of ice. Suck'em up. It was his going-away-to-college party. And he had this girl, a girl from your high school. Remember? What was her name?

I drank five cups of punch, and when I couldn't stand up, I drank on my hands and knees, like a dog, out of the cooler. You said we had to learn how to smoke, you said all men smoke cigars, and you gave me your pocketknife, the red one with the white cross, and long, fat cigar. Cut off the end, you said. When we lit it, it smelled like hair burning. Or a piece of rope. The smoke made my head spin. I had to lie on my back, next to the cooler, to keep from spinning off the world. When you went to the bathroom, I threw the cigar in the punch, and put your knife in my pocket. That's when I heard Dafun on the porch, telling the girl he wasn't a virgin and she wasn't a virgin so what the hell. She said he was a jerk. And he kept talking, saying he was going to be gone the next day, to college. Somehow, I managed to walk out there, spinning, trying to find my slippers, and I said, Hey. I was really spinning. Hey, I said, don't talk like that, to her.

He was about two inches taller than me and really pissed off. I couldn't see him through the spinning. He got in my face. He sad something like What the suck. Then the girl grabbed his shoulder and told him to leave me alone. Leave him alone, she said. Hey, I said, still spinning. I should've busted him but I didn't want to throw the first punch, and I didn't know if it would reach him. Dafun nailed me good. Remember? I crashed into you and you nailed Dafun and the next I remember, I was staring at my feet. I was wearing black slippers, on the wrong feet.

I remember that girl. She had black earrings. A black pearl in each ear. She sat between us in the VW. Your hand touched her knee when you shifted into fourth. There was blood on your knuckles. She talked about how she wanted to be a teacher. I told her we didn't want to be anything. We were going to Hawaii.

What about Vietnam? she said.

We had the windows down to help us stay awake, and we were getting cold. A swim to sober up, you said, your hands on the steering wheel.

What about the war? she said.

I found a flashlight in the glove compartment. No need, you said, the moon's full. There was a blanket and a flashlight in the trunk. I went first, across the sand. When she stepped on a piece of glass, you pulled it out. A drop of blood appeared on her sole, and you pressed hard with your finger until it stopped. Then you carried her to the darkness. I sat near the water, dreaming of a place where the water would be warm enough for midnight swims. The air would smell of eucalyptus trees and library books and perfume.

I dug my toes into the sand and dreamed of you and her swimming through the surf. We could see the coral reef below gently dropping down to a hundred feet. She grabbed my foot. We're flying, she said, we're flying over castles. While you swam on your back, laughing, I dove to the bottom, and when I looked up, she swam over me. I let out all my breath, bubbles rising to her, umbrellas going up. I wanted her to dive down to me. I felt her shadow touch my chest She put her hand on your shoulder.

I waited. Dreaming. I closed my eyes. She kissed me. She pressed her body against me, and water rushed into my lungs, past black pearls in her ears.

When the two of you came back, I said, A mermaid swam over me.

178

You laughed at that. That's a good one, you said. Only in your dreams, you said.

She knelt in the sand and kissed the salt from my eyes. She wrote her phone number on the sleeve of your letterman's jacket. I wonder where she is now. Remember?

What happened, David?

At the end of the night, you said you were never going home. We watched cars pass on the freeway. The pale morning, half sunrise, half streetlight, reminded me of cotton candy. The lemon pickers wore straw hats that hid their faces. A woman smoking a short cigar looked at us as she climbed onto the company truck. You said you were never going home.

Remember?

The letter you wrote my mother said you were doing an important job, said I'd straighten out soon. One night I almost froze to death, in a T-shirt and a pair of jeans, hiding in a telephone booth near the Canadian border. I slept sitting with my arms wrapped around my knees and woke with my legs stiff. I couldn't walk.

They brought you home, to bury you in a small cemetery near the freeway. Before the funeral, I cut my hand with your pocketknife, to see blood. Tasted it. I stood over your grave. Your father said, "He did what he had to do. He was a man."

I remember you as a boy on a bicycle.

David, I was supposed to die with you.

Now, I see my face in black granite. I live outside of town and do not talk about you. People wouldn't understand. They'd say you were a hero. Or that I did the right thing. I've been married and divorced. My ex-wife lives close to here. We're still friends. She's married, has two children, a boy and a girl. I've worked as a dishwasher, a gardener, a carpenter. In the mornings now I walk barefoot over slippery rocks looking for glass balls incoming on the tide. On Friday nights I drink beer and watch television until my head falls back on the couch. I wake up feeling old.

Today I feel as if I'm eighteen, as if I never grew up. Is that possible? For me to stay eighteen all my life, my outside growing older and my inside staying young. Sometimes, I hear people talking, then stillness.

I keep too many things. I have a monopoly game and a shoebox full of old swimming medals. I have pieces of a novel I tried to write about a man who runs a shop called Something Better, where people go to buy new lives.

I have to stop for a minute. I'm tired. It's the heat. I'm going to kneel, to be closer to you. At first, I couldn't find your name. I had to ask directions. There are over fifty-eight thousand names cut in polished black granite. They are listed in chronological order by date of death, from 1959 to 1975. The average age is nineteen. The honor guard has a book with the names listed alphabetically. They point to a wall section and line number for each name. People bring flowers, their petals are red, and white, and yellow. Along the wall beneath the names, there's a can of beer, a new spool of fishing line, a picture of a boy standing next to his father.

In the black granite, I can see my face. I can touch the letters of your name. The air is filled with the smell of memories. Do you remember me? I am alive now, here, alone, in paradise.

18. axle of evil

When people in Hilo see me, usually they ask about my old pal, Johnny, the lolo auto mechanic. Johnny works cheap and knows cars, but he's slightly twisted, and he's highly contagious.

Of course, no one warned me about him. Hilo people are friendly as hell, and they'll spend two hours talking about how hot it is or how their daughter won the spelling bee at St. Joe's, but then they forget the important stuff, like, "You're building your house in a flood zone!" or "Johnny, dat buggah, no can hear straight."

The first time I ran into Johnny, I was trying to coax the last few miles out of my '68 VW Bug. It's my wife's favorite car, but the rear end was grinding so bad, I was headed for the landfill, thinking I'd dump the Bug first and explain later. I was turning onto the dirt road that led to the landfill when I saw big red sign splashed onto the side of a rusting Quonset hut: "David, the barefoot mechanic. Make your car problems a memory."

So I coasted down a steep driveway, and found a tall boy stretched out behind a metal desk, popping M&Ms and washing them down with hits from a 92-ounce Big Gulp. He took a quick look under my rear end and said, "Hell, you got one of them axles of evil!"

Before I could say anything, he grabbed a fat wrench, slid under the VW, and banged away at the axle, shouting at me how the Saddom-o-mites are working to get axles of evil into every VW and Ford and Sony flat screen from here to Canada, which is a country north of Wal-mart, and if we don't take action, we'll be forced to watch reruns of Oprah and wear Levis made in China and stand in long lines barefoot so old ladies can get their social security checks x-rayed.

The banging stopped, and he shouted, "See?"

The only thing I saw was camouflaged shorts, hairy man legs, and big heavy combat boots sticking out from under my VW.

He went back to banging and shouting. "The only way to beat these Saddam-o-mites is to hit them with Smart Bombs. See, they got everything backward. They think we're the problem, but we know they're the problem, so we got to make-em smarter, more self-reflective. A long time ago we learned that regular bombs are no good. Regular bombing is like kicking a dog, over and over, with a steel boot. Sooner or later that dog bites back, goes radioactive Martha Stewart on your behind."

For some reason, mention of dogs biting back made me thinking of the hand-painted sign on the Quonset hut, "Hey, David," I said, "you sure you know what you're doing?"

He pops out, and up—hair flying crazy, like Einstein on crack—and stands an inch from face, still holding that wrench. "David?" he said. "You seen David?"

"I thought you were David."

"No, I'm Johnny." He glanced at the M&M's on the desk. He looked out the window at the landfill. Then he slipped back under the VW. All real slow, like he was swimming in a dream. "David's gone," he said.

I heard more banging, then he started up again.

"Smart bombs are packed with IQ enhancers. You drop a smart bomb on a dog, it doesn't bite, it smiles and says. 'Now I understand. I want to be just like you.' We got Smart Bombs full of IQ enhancers, you know, clips from Joe Millionaire, and Girls Gone Wild in Hilo, and pictures of strip malls and strippers and fly strips, and Rush Limbaugh with a goatee getting married to Anna Nicole Smith. See, and we drop these smart bombs, and before you know it, the Saddom-o-mites have given up Saddom-o-miting, and they're eating low-fat hamburgers, living in the suburbs, and voting for Bud or Bud-light. War ain't like it used to be. It's kinder and gentler and more Democratic."

I'm about to ask for my car back but, he's out and up and standing in front of me before I can say anything. He grabs my hand, shakes it hard. "This VW will keep running, believe me. I'm an optimist. Just stay close to home. Whatever you do, don't try to leave Hilo."

He had worker hands, wiry and strong, thick and calloused. I reached for my wallet, but he said, "No charge. It's on me and David. David drove a VW. You'll see. The world's getting better. Peace, brother."

From what I saw over the next few months, the world didn't get a whole lot better. It turned rainy and wet, then hot and dry, then back to rainy and wet. It rained for 30 days straight, but my VW kept running. Maybe it would have run forever, but on the Tuesday after Veteran's Day it rained so hard I cracked and headed up Saddle Road, aimed at the sliver of sunshine over Kona. The VW was purring and climbing, winding up the volcano. Clouds were rushing by. The chill was driving out the rain. Then, exactly one mile out of Hilo, the rear end choked, coughed, choked again. I turned on the radio to blot out the noise, but the radio choked too, and started speaking in tongues. One voice was saying, "Hello, this is Governor Linda Lingle, education," and behind her was a man's voice saying "Something going to happen, be scared, code flaming red. Be scared" and behind him were the Rolling Stones singing "Look out for your 19th nervous breakdown."

Lucky for me, it was a downhill run back to Johnny's place.

I found him sitting in the cool shadows of the Quonset hut, all quiet staring out the window at the landfill, like he's a kid in love and the mountain of rusting cars is an ocean sunset and somewhere out in that rusting red mess is his sweetheart. I was thinking maybe he's better and he won't be saying anything bad about Martha Stewart, but then he looked at me and said, "It's happening again. All over. I keep seeing his bare feet."

I looked at his feet. He was still wearing his combat boots, the jungle boot kind from Vietnam days. He said, "We were young then, just out of high school, me and David. That was a long time ago. I wish I couldn't remember, but I still see him. He drove a 57 Bug that had one of those tiny black wheels instead of a gas pedal and he drove barefoot. He could fix that car, he could fix any car. He was a chunky kid but strong and smart. A lifeguard. One day he swam out in ten-foot surf to rescue a kid, no jet ski rescues back then, only rip currents and water churned brown and black. That's how I remember him, waves lifting him up, then dropping him down, him disappearing into the trough. The kid he was trying to rescue was out there, waving, bobbing, drifting. David grabbed him, strapped him into the orange rescue tube, and plowed back, each wave smashing the two of them into an avalanche of white. I thought both of them were going to drown but I was too scared to help. David never said nothing about that to me. He just acted like what I did, which was nothing, was the most natural thing in the world.

"One night we drank a gallon of red wine and smoked five cigars, stubby ones, long ones, big fat ones. Until we were spinning, spread out on the grass, staring up at the stars, the world spinning underneath us. He told me he wasn't waiting for the draft, he wanted to get out of town, see the world."

Johnny looked at me and said, "Have you seen him?"

Me, I was lost, breathing scratchy vog mixed with rubbish fumes and wondering why the hell I had made the same mistake twice.

Johnny said, "Guys like you don't understand. You just drive around carefree, drinking beer, getting tattoos, laughing it up, no one tells you to be a man, do your duty. You got gas pedals and shoes."

I couldn't argue with that.

He said, "Have you ever loved a man? I mean, have you ever lost someone and missed him so bad, missed him so bad you can smell him, smell the salt water on his skin? Missed him so bad, you could sit in one place and play the same record over and over again, thinking about him and back in the days?"

He was looking out the window, facing the landfill. "It's happening again," he said. "The boys are leaving home, brave all of them. Heroes. Bodies in the street, mothers crying over broken children. All of it, the glory, the mission, the freedom covered in thick red blood, the flags flying, and David, in that VW driving barefoot with his toes wrapped around the little black wheel."

I looked out the window where he's looking but didn't see any of those things, just rusting refrigerators and wrecked cars and old batteries dripping acid.

I left my VW at Johnny's and walked home, figuring I'd never have to deal with Johnny again because that old bug was history. Then, later that same day, I got a call from my wife. Somehow Johnny had gotten hold of her, and she had gone down to pick up the VW. Him and her had talked for a long time, which kind of surprised me because my wife is a lawyer and time is money and she doesn't like to waste time, but now she was driving the bug home, and telling me on her cell phone how she saved my VW and how Mr. Sheshe died.

It took me a second because I didn't know any Mr. Sheshe except the homeless guy who lived in Kalakaua Park. He got his name from peeing whenever he feels the need, no matter where he is, no matter who is around, but I had never heard my wife say much about him, except maybe, "Damn that Mr. Sheshe."

Now my wife was telling me, through the cell-phone haze and VW engine noise, "Mr. Sheshe died on Veterans Day in Kalakaua Park, on a bench facing the federal building, the one with white columns. From my office window I saw him sit down with a brown paper bag between his knees. He took a long drink, swallowed, then looked up at me. I saw his lips move, saying what he always says to me. 'Hello sistah, you looking good today.' Mr. Sheshe died on Veteran's day, in the morning when the air was still wet from the night's rain, and down the street from the mountain, cars came, bright red in the sunrise.

"The night before, I caught him standing in the doorway of the law firm, the office built in 1931, peeing a long stream of Colt 45 and Budweiser, the rain falling on his back, his hair hidden under a wool cap.

"I yelled at him to stop. To get out. Now he's dead. Did you know he was a veteran of the Korean War? He died on Veterans Day, on a park bench, under a newspaper with headlines warning about the war in Baghdad.

"Can you hear me?" she said. "Do you hear me?"

I heard her, but I didn't know what to say. I was thinking about Johnny and David, the two of them in that old VW, David driving barefoot. I was thinking that people in Hilo are friendly as hell, and I wanted my wife home, safe in my arms, a thousand, million miles away from the killing, so we could talk about the kid who won the spelling bee at St. Joe's.

19. buried in vermeer's light

"The first night in town, I heard two shots."

Start before that.

Manny glanced at blank walls, watched a tiny flag move into harsh light. Stars and stripes burning bright, Manny wanted to do right. "When Billy put me on the plane in Honolulu, he warned me to stay out of Amsterdam. Take the train straight to Maastricht and don't talk to anybody."

Why'd he say that?

"Billie's always joking. I only speak English, who am I going to talk to?"

Tell us about the woman.

Manny remembered the taxi ride across the river, past city walls, onto a quiet street lined with Dutch elms. He climbed narrow steps, three at a time, to a studio where huge windows poured moonlight. Not the light he was searching for but good light. In this pale glow, filtered through cloudy glass that reminded him of his grandfather's house, he heard two shots.

Tell us about the woman.

While he struggled with the window's heavy brass handle, trying to work it like a beer tap, he saw wavy trees, brick buildings nearly hidden behind ivy-covered walls, then a woman on a bicycle, wearing a flowing dress that exposed flashes, flashes of white as she pedaled in the moonlight.

Tell us about the woman.

In the morning, she knocked once. While he was listening to Billie say that the writer would be a few days late, her mother sick, she knocked again. He was supposed to take background shots, fill them with color...

He lost the connection as she let herself in, saying sorry, sorry, not much English. Wearing pointy shoes and a loose dress, she turned the dial on the washing machine, twice so he could see, pointed at the rubbish cans, one for paper, one for glass, one for other...things. she showed him how to push the window latch up, then down. Warm light rushed in. Now, he could see loops of barbed-wire on the brick wall, and further down a narrow gate, where a soldier with a clipboard checked license plates.

Where did you meet her?

In a sidewalk café, around the corner in the park, where he had gone to watch World Cup soccer and drink dark beer. In hundred degree heat, Holland was losing to Portugal. Men and women stripped to bathing suits, sat on yellow grass. As cars drove by, children pointed at goats ad reindeer in the zoo. Under a blue umbrella, shaded from the bright light, he dipped a tiny square of dark bread into olive oil, washed it down with Gulpener, Gladiator, 10% alcohol. He pushed his finger on a map, over a walking bridge, a library, a museum as a young woman walked by, child on hip, feet kicking, small hands gripping her loose dress. She paused to take a breath, before hurrying by a soldier guarding a narrow gate.

Tell us about the woman.

From far away, the Bonnefante, a Dutch museum designed by an Italian, looked liked a four-story bullet pointed at the sky. Inside, on wood floors she stood next to him while he stared at a girl painted with a pearl earring, and a digital voice whispered in his ear. "In the painting of Vermeer in particular, we can see the fundamental characteristics of Dutch painting, love of light and the common human experience of everyday life, brought to their highest levels of artistic expression." He felt her walk behind him, felt a soft wave of cool air brush against his neck, and heard the taped voice whisper, "The girl looks over her shoulder, suggesting that the viewer is the one who has made the girl turn her head."

On a narrow road along the river, on a bike rented near the train station, in light that reminded him of late afternoon in Hilo Town, he pedaled past men sitting in folding chairs, watching long fishing poles, as river barges cut through still waters, and he thought of the Ala Wai, and his father's friends fishing for tilapia.

Until he was lost.

Where had the road taken him? Outside the walled the city, into farmland, stretches of new wheat. The canal reflected trees, people moving in and out of barges, afternoon meals spread on picnic tables. The air, thick and heavy with pollen, carried the promise of diesel fuel and allergies.

In the opposite direction, a grey-haired woman pedaled, sitting straight, handlebar basket filled with sunflowers. And he turned, thinking he had seen her before, followed her, recognizing a church, a small bridge, before he wondered about rows of modern apartments, a video store, and found himself at the entrance to a cemetery, where she had locked her bike.

Was she his neighbor, the woman who lived alone? The one who caught him by his door in the morning when it was cool, taking her dog for a walk, and said her son was in Afghanistan?

Camera in hand, he followed her on shaded paths, stopped to meter moss-covered gravestones from 1742, then a mausoleum with a candlelit altar, a gate almost rusted shut. He walked past graves marked 1942, 1943, 1944, 1944. Words in Hebrew and Dutch. The woman placed sunflowers on a boxed-shaped monument, waist high, made of marble. When she walked away, not looking back, into shadowed lanes, stretching endlessly through tall trees, offering tempting light, he stood where she had stood. Arm sun on the back of his neck, he heard wind in the trees, read Dutch, then Hebrew, then English: "In memory of the Jewish children of Maastricht that were lead to perish in the concentration camps in the years 1940-1945."

The light shifted, bright to his face.

You said the woman was an accident.

He wondered when he had started counting graves. He remembered sitting on the bench facing the American cemetery at Margarten. His grandfather's friend was buried there. He sat in the sun, counting the graves, waiting for the light to change so he could photograph the names on the wall. He pushed his finger over the engraved name Sasaoka Itsumu, Staff Sergeant 442 Infantry Regiment, wondering if the Hawaii boy missed the light falling over the Pali. The warm granite reminded him of the wall in DC, where his father's friends, now only names, were imprisoned in dark reflections that absorbed all light.

Tell us about the woman.

She sat across from him on the train, a young woman with a pearl earring, who spoke English. He thought it an accident, some sort of odd coincidence that brought her to him. He told her he had come to Holland looking for the right light. She blinked twice. Light, he said, that makes people see angles yet is soft and sharp at the same time, so a flat object seemed round and full. He said Holland was famous for its light. She said really and talked about palm trees and volcanoes and how Bruddah Iz was big in Amsterdam.

The countryside flashed by in train windows.

He told her his idea that people in Hawaii were the same, same as people in Holland, how they both liked to drink beer and sit in the sun and eat and talk and fish.

She told him she had studied economics at the university in Rotterdam, had quit to avoid becoming one of them, ended up in the Sudan, setting up a trade show. She looked away for a moment then turned back to him, said she was proud of doing the work herself. The little Dutch girl. Now she was going to visit her brother....

The conductor pushed through the door.

"... in the prison, where the Americans keep the terrorists."

He wondered about the missing words, lost somewhere as the conductor checked their tickets, then moved by in a black uniform, trailing cigarette smell, interrupting windows filled with fields of wheat.

She smiled, rubbed her chin. When the train hit a rough spot, they both reached to steady their bikes, and he said he was going to the national monument, the concentration camp.

She knew the place. Did he know the way?

A coincidence.

She would take him there. It was next to the prison.

The bicycle route led along the canal, splitting fields from shady groves. She rushed ahead of him, looked back, called I thought you Americans were strong. They passed a sign in English—Stay Out!—with a picture of a German Shepard. Stay out!

They walked along the edges of sandy woods, on trails of thick sand. She said she couldn't imagine it, living in the middle of an ocean.

Neither could he.

She pointed at a path across a stream, said that's where the Dutch resistance where shot by the Dutch guards The camp was just on the other side of the trees. They had come the back way to avoid the busy streets.

He thought of the ocean.

Why did you come here?

Searching for Vermeer's light.

At the gate, the attendant, a slim young man in slacks and a dress shirt, smiled and handed him the last brochure in English: National Monument Camp Vught. "Roughly sixty years after the liberation of the camps, the premises are still in use. The southern and eastern part by the Dutch military service, the middle houses the free Moluccans who sided with the Dutch in Indonesia in the middle 1950s and wait for a time when they can return. The northern part is the property of the Dutch Department of Justice."

Start in the restaurant. Follow the arrows. Through the audio-visual section where you can see and hear the survivors. In its early years, the camp was used as a workplace for Phillips. Yes, the one that makes TVs. There was a hospital, a barracks, a dormitory. Through there, you'll find Cell 115 – 9 square meters – where 74 women were locked up for 14 hours. Through there the crematorium, and out the door to the children's monument.

Here, "on the 6th of June of 1943, all children of 0-4 years old were rounded up and taken to the railway station where the cattle wagons were waiting for them. The train went, with a short stop at the Jewish transit-camp Westerbrork, straight in to the gas-chambers of Sorbidor. The next day all the children from 4 up to 16 followed to the same destination. Within a couple of days 1260 children were murdered as well as the 1800 parents who were allowed to join them. The youngest victim was six days old."

He found his memory next to the crematorium, next to eight pillars topped with Jewish stars. At the base, a bronze teddy bear, a baby doll, a pile of books.

Tell us about the woman

He heard their cries.

Thought of blue water, the ocean between them, thought of Hawaii and this place, counting graves.

You were seen with her on the train.

On the train.

Manny glanced at blank walls, watched a tiny flag pinned to a lapel reflect harsh light. Stars and stripes burning bright. They had taken his camera and passport.

"The first night in town I heard two shots. Small caliber pistol shots."

Start before that.

"When Billy put me on the plane in Honolulu, he warned me to stay out of Amsterdam. Take the train straight to Maastricht, don't talk to anybody."

Why'd he say that?

There were two of them, men in suits, one Dutch, one American. The Dutch cop dug in his pocket, found a stainless steel Zippo.

"The first night in town I heard two shots."

They spread his photographs on the table, the shots of the prison wall, the guard tower, the barbed wire.

Why'd you take these pictures?

"I work for a magazine."

What kind of magazine?

The Dutch guy slipped an unfiltered Camel into his mouth, flicked open the lighter, stopped when the American gave him a sideways glance. Stars and stripes burning bright. It was not the light Manny was looking for.

A guy like you, a veteran, you must understand why we ask these questions. It's a new world since 9…

There was nothing new about this world. Manny sat on the bench facing the river, in the shadow of the concrete wall that separated a maximum-security prison from a bronze teddy bear. Jewish stars burning bright. Manny watched the countryside flash by in train windows. Manny walked beside the rows of soldiers buried in Vermeer's light.

Why'd you come here?

Manny refused to speak, sat instead, counting graves.

Writer's Note
The quoted description of Camp Vught and the children's death is taken from the "English Guide, National Monument Camp Vught, 2004."

20. magic words in the
palace of desire

Patsy inhaled the salty, sweet scent of tears, shifted her weight, and leaped onto the cluttered desk. Her front claws rested at the edge of a crumpled note.

Dear Lover,

I have to ask a favor. I love you, and you're a good man, so please understand. We can't live in the Palace forever. I want children and we need a home. I signed the papers, so it's my duty. It can't last forever. We'll be together soon. Please understand. And please, please take care of the cats!

Love always,

The girl

Patsy stared at the words, trying to understand. Last night the woman had sat here writing. This morning the man sat here crying. What did it mean? She jumped off the desk and ran up the stairs to the balcony. The man was sitting alone in the back row, in the shadowy light that made humans eat popcorn and hold hands. On the torn screen, a flat man and woman stood in the rain, the woman clutching a flat baby to her breast. When the train behind them puffed smoke, the couple grabbed each other and touched lips.

Patsy smelled her woman's jasmine perfume, felt something inside her missing. On the screen, the flat woman was running alongside her man as he boarded the train, calling out to her, "I love you. I love you."

For humans, these words could perform magic. Patsy tried to shape the words with her mouth, managed an extended squeak, and almost instantly saw the man on the screen leap forward in time and off the train. Now he was pointing a rifle at men in mud houses while explosions kicked up dirt and smoke. Patsy did not like loud noises, so she skittered down the aisle, past rows of seats, to a narrow space behind the broken pipe organ, where she found Ernie sleeping in his favorite bed, a ragged violin case.

She stared at him, willing him to wake, so close to his tiny grey nose, she could smell his dreams of skillet fried ahi and braised opakapaka. "Love," she whispered.

Magically, Ernie opened his deep green eyes. Half in the world of flickering movie light, he blinked, half in the world of flakey white fish sautéed in red wine and butter.

Patsy tapped his nose with her paw, darted away, stopped, glanced back.

Ernie liked the chase game. Even though he could never remember the endings, he knew all the beginnings. As Patsy slipped behind the curtain, he leaped onto the stage. Stopped. Stretched. Followed her into the darkness, down the stairs, through the hole cut in the corrugated tin. Where was she?

Moonlight and misty rain fell on an abandoned car, an over-stuffed dumpster.

To cover his surprise, Ernie sat down, blinked. How could she have disappeared so quickly? Disappearing was his specialty. A shorthair, pure gray, with extra long legs, he could run faster than any cat in Hilo, blend into shadows, hide in the tiniest places. Even back in the day, when he was a kitten at the Keaau Animal Shelter, he could make himself invisible. Only the woman had been able to find him and her only because Patsy had leaped out of her arms and refused to leave without the tiny gray shadow huddled in the corner.

Patsy was different. Part Siamese, part something else, she had presence. The beach cats called her a mini-tanker, because she was big enough to carry a load but small enough to crank a sharp turn. The thick brown fur on her back kept the rain off, the white underneath made her look like clouds passing, and her shadowy mask made her intense blue eyes seem even more intense. No matter where she went, the thick humans bent to pet her, to call her beautiful, or to point at the cute white spot on the tip of her tail.

But where was she?

Behind the dumpster, Patsy stopped at Angelina the Calico's home. She was sleeping in the corner next to the drainpipe, with six tiny kittens lined up at her nipples. Patsy felt the kittens nibbling at her breasts, felt their tiny mouths sucking her skin. Where did they come from? Many times, Patsy had seen the humans at the Palace hugging and whispering and saying the magic words, and then babies would appear.

She crept close to a tiny orange female who had been pushed away from its mother's breast, smelled its neck, its milky sweet breath, nudged her back into her mother's thick fur. Patsy licked the glistening raindrops off the kitten's tail.

Again, she felt something inside her missing.

In her younger days, Patsy had felt the same missing. Restless beyond belief, she had spent long nights in the bamboo forest across from the jail and in the park behind the Suisan dock, where the rats were as big as cats and the dumpsters were piled high with tasty scraps from the Hilo Hawaiian breakfast buffet. She had stolen rides in the woman's truck, tasted malasadas in Honokaa and chased cats fat from beer-batter fish and chips in Kona. Trying to quench the thirst that would not leave her, she had drunk the coppery-ash water of Volcano.

In the parking lot next to St. Joseph's, she had let the males chase her, then stood her ground, and they had backed off, went back to their humans singing about a place called heaven. She had challenged the cats behind the jail, and by the river, and in the alley behind Pesto's, the ones who slept late and spent their nights grinning and swinging their tails to the rhythm of jazz. She preferred the big ones best, the ones who smelled of spilled wine and bacon grease, but none of them had been able to change her, to make her more than one.

Now that the woman was gone, Patsy felt the same emptiness. She leaned close to the kitten. Its breath in her ear reminded her of the woman's whispers, saying the magic words, I love you, I love you. Patsy tried the words again, but no kittens moved inside her.

She heard him a second before. Big Brad landed on the wet concrete. He was a big cat, nearly twenty-five pounds. A Siamese mix, a cane cat with a huge head and stubby tail, most of his weight was in his shoulders, and his thick fur was spotted with chicken grease and tuna oil. He had a busted claw and an aching back, but he lived by the rules. This pretty female from the Palace had been touching his kittens. He had chased her before, and he would chase her again. Now his eyes searched her eyes, felt her blue-eyed stare.

Patsy darted to the nearest shadow, stopped, rubbed slowly, slowly along corrugated tin. She did not know why she did these things. She did them automatically, saying under her breath, I love you, I love you, wanting the woman back.

She felt his weight on her, felt his teeth in her neck. Saw the kittens sucking on Angelina's nipples. Love, she said, love. Felt his weight pressing her to the wet concrete.

Invisible, Ernie slipped along the dry strip under the eaves of the Palace, a shadow moving in and out of the spaces between the rubbish cans. He was thinking about the woman's incredibly delicate hands, and how she knew the exact spot on his neck that needed constant attention, rubbing and petting. She had impressed him with her dedication, her ability to sit long hours with Patsy on her lap. She had an endless supply of energy and could play wrestling games with the man all through the night, then wake in the morning and play wrestling with him again. Every day she cleaned the Palace, stocked the kitchen with tuna, and heated the popcorn humans liked to eat in darkness.

He was about to give up the search and go home, when he heard a female crying. At least it sounded like crying, the kind of crying Angelina the Calico had done before her kittens ap-peared. Then he smelled something familiar, a jasmine smell, and something oily. A scruffy black tail protruded from behind the dumpster. Big Brad's tail. Ernie did not want to meet Big Brad in a dark alley, but as he turned to run, Patsy's white tip appeared, tangled with the bruiser's stub.

Still in the shadows, he stepped closer. Was this how the game was supposed to end? Patsy cried as if someone were pressing the life out of her. Even though Ernie was not a fighter, he whispered his war cry, the one he used to keep mice and small cats away from the Palace, whispered again. Then he saw Patsy pinned to the ground, under Big Brad's huge mess of sticky hair. Ernie growled his louder, deeper throatier territorial growl. As Patsy cried, Big Brad pressed her neck to the ground. Ernie dove for him, lost his footing, but managed to sink his teeth into the soft skin under Big Brad's front leg. He bit and held. There was nothing else to do. Ernie was not a heavy cat. He was long and fast, with hooked claws for climbing, but now he bit down and held tight, rode the flying, leaping, twisting bundle of fur. Patsy popped free.

Ernie twisted, turned, kicked at Brad's stomach, felt his lungs being crushed by the big cat's weight. Was this how the game was supposed to end? To take his mind off the pain, Ernie dreamed of far off places. At the exact moment that Big Brad managed to twist around and get hold of Ernie's throat, at this exact moment of intense physical pain, Ernie was thinking of the dumpster behind Blane's, two blocks up from the Palace, where a smart cat could always find scraps of katsu chicken or gravy burger.

Was this how the game was supposed to end?

Patsy flew at Brad's back, threw her weight at him, knocking him off balance. She had tiny claws but she had weight, that is how she killed mynah birds, crushed them. She knocked Brad against the dumpster, shoved hard until Ernie popped free.

Patsy stood her ground. Hissed. Ernie shot across the alley and landed at the door to the Palace. In a blink of intense blue eyes, Patsy twisted, slapped a claw across Brad's nose, whispered I love you, and magically disappeared into the darkness, leaving behind only the memory of a brilliant white spot.

***

Ernie sat in the front row and licked his wound while he watched the humans on the screen. Long ago, Ernie had learned not to trust these flat people. They were prone to sudden movements. There was no telling what they would do, or when they would do it. Now there were two of them, a flat man and woman sitting in a movie theater eating popcorn and looking at him, as if he were the movie. This was too confusing for Ernie. He limped up the aisle to the balcony and hopped into the empty seat next to his man.

The flat man on the screen said to the flat woman, "When I was younger, I dreamed of far off places, coffee shops in Amsterdam, art galleries in Paris, doing crazy things. But I stayed at home."

Patsy leaped effortlessly, settled next to Ernie, the two of them together in one seat. On the screen the flat humans were touching lips.

Patsy looked at Ernie. Three years old, he still had a baby face and smelled of moldy leather. The two of them had lived together in the animal shelter, had been taken together to the pet hospital for their operations. She tried to image him chasing her, pinning her to the ground, touching her, doing the things humans did on the screen and in the balcony after eating too much popcorn.

She heard his heavy breathing, whispered, "I love you."

Ernie kept his eyes on the flat humans. Any second, they might break out in song or produce a flat baby. They needed constant watching.

The man leaned over and stroked Patsy's neck, whispered, "Don't you worry, girl. I'll take care of you." His hand smelled of jasmine perfume.

The screen was going black.

Patsy wondered if Ernie had tasted opihi caught on the cliffs at Onomea, the margaritas behind Reuben's. She licked a drop of blood off his ear, whispered, "I love you."

Ernie blinked. He liked the chase game.

www.ingramcontent.com/pod-product-compliance
Lightning Source LLC
Chambersburg PA
CBHW020406150626
46554CB00012B/388